AT THE ALTAR

Forbidden Courtship

"Look here, Burton," said old John Ellis in an ominous tone of voice, "I want to know if what that old busybody of a Mary Keane came here today gossiping about is true. If it is — well, I've something to say about the matter! Have you been courting that niece of Susan Oliver's all summer on the sly?"

Burton Ellis's handsome, boyish face flushed darkly crimson to the roots of his curly black hair. Something in the father's tone roused anger and rebellion in the son. He straightened himself up from the turnip row he was hoeing, looked his father squarely in the face, and said quietly, "Not on the sly, sir. I never do things that way. But I have been going to see Madge Oliver for some time, and we are engaged. We are thinking of being married this fall, and we hope you will not object."

Burton's frankness nearly took away his father's breath. Old John fairly choked with rage.

"You young fool," he spluttered, bringing down his hoe with such energy that he sliced off half a dozen of his finest young turnip plants, "have you gone clean crazy? No, sir, I'll never consent to your marrying an Oliver, and you needn't have any idea that I will."

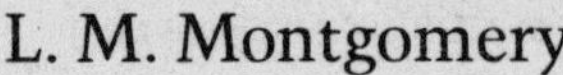

L. M. Montgomery

At the Altar

MATRIMONIAL TALES

edited by Rea Wilmshurst

BANTAM BOOKS
NEW YORK • TORONTO • LONDON • SYDNEY • AUCKLAND

RL 6.5, age 012 and up

AT THE ALTAR

A Bantam Book / published by arrangement with
McClelland & Stewart Inc.

The Starfire logo is a registered trademark of Bantam Books, a division of Bantam Doubleday Dell Publishing Group, Inc.
Registered in U.S. Patent and Trademark Office and elsewhere.

Bantam edition/June 1995

For information address: McClelland & Stewart Inc., 481 University Avenue, Toronto, Ontario M5G 2E9 Canada.

ISBN 0-553-56748-9

Published simultaneously in the United States and Canada

Bantam Books are published by Bantam Books, a division of Bantam Doubleday Dell Publishing Group, Inc. Its trademark, consisting of the words "Bantam Books" and the portrayal of a rooster, is Registered in U.S. Patent and Trademark Office and in other countries. Marca Registrada. Bantam Books, 1540 Broadway, New York, New York 10036.

PRINTED IN THE UNITED STATES OF AMERICA

OPM 0 9 8 7 6 5 4 3

Contents

Aunt Philippa and the Men

KNEW quite well why Father sent me to Prince Edward Island to visit Aunt Philippa that summer. He told me he was sending me there "to learn some sense"; and my stepmother, of whom I was very fond, told me she was sure the sea air would do me a world of good. I did not want to learn sense or be done a world of good; I wanted to stay in Montreal and go on being foolish – and make up my quarrel with Mark Fenwick. Father and Mother did not know anything about this quarrel; they thought I was still on good terms with him – and that is why they sent me to Prince Edward Island.

I was very miserable. I did not want to go to Aunt Philippa's. It was not because I feared it would be dull – for without Mark, Montreal was just as much of a howling wilderness as any other place. But it was so horribly far away. When the time came for Mark to want to make up – as come I knew it would – how could he do it if I were seven hundred miles away?

Nevertheless, I went to Prince Edward Island. In all my eighteen years I had never once disobeyed Father. He is a very hard man to disobey. I knew I should have to make a beginning some time if I wanted to marry Mark, so I saved all my little courage up for that and didn't waste any of it opposing the visit to Aunt Philippa.

I couldn't understand Father's point of view. Of course, he hated old John Fenwick, who had once sued him for libel and won the case. Father had written an indiscreet editorial in the excitement of a red-hot political contest – and was made to understand that there are some things you can't say of another man even at election time. But then, he need not have hated Mark because of that; Mark was not even born when it happened.

Old John Fenwick was not much better pleased about Mark and me than Father was, though he didn't go to the length of forbidding it; he just acted grumpily and disagreeably. Things were unpleasant enough all round without a quarrel between Mark and me; yet quarrel we did – and over next to nothing, too, you understand. And now I had to set out for Prince Edward Island without even seeing him, for he was away in Toronto on business.

WHEN MY TRAIN REACHED COPELY the next afternoon, Aunt Philippa was waiting for me. There was nobody else in sight, but I would have known her had there been a thousand. Nobody but Aunt Philippa could have that determined mouth, those piercing grey eyes, and that pronounced, unmistakable Goodwin nose. And certainly nobody but Aunt Philippa would have come to meet me arrayed in a wrapper of chocolate print with huge yellow roses scattered over it, and a striped blue-and-white apron!

She welcomed me kindly but absent-mindedly, her thoughts evidently being concentrated on the problem of getting my trunk home. I had only the one, and in Montreal it had seemed to be of moderate size; but on the platform of Copely station, sized up by Aunt Philippa's merciless eye, it certainly looked huge.

"I thought we could a-took it along tied on the back of the buggy," she said disapprovingly, "but I guess we'll have to leave it, and I'll send the hired boy over for it tonight. You can get along without it till then, I s'pose?"

There was a fine irony in her tone. I hastened to assure her meekly that I could, and that it did not matter if my trunk could not be taken up till next day.

"Oh, Jerry can come for it tonight as well as not," said Aunt Philippa, as we climbed into her buggy. "I'd a good notion to send him to meet you, for he isn't doing much today, and I wanted to go to Mrs. Roderick MacAllister's funeral. But my head was aching me so bad I thought I wouldn't enjoy the funeral if I did go. My head is better now, so I kind of wish I had gone. She was a hundred and four years old and I'd always promised myself that I'd go to her funeral."

Aunt Philippa's tone was melancholy. She did not recover her good spirits until we were out on the pretty, grassy, elm-shaded country road, garlanded with its ribbon of buttercups. Then she suddenly turned around and looked me over scrutinizingly.

"You're not as good-looking as I expected from your picture, but them photographs always flatter. That's the reason I never had any took. You're rather thin and brown. But you've good eyes and you look clever. Your father writ me you hadn't much sense, though. He wants me to teach you some, but it's a thankless business. People would rather be fools."

Aunt Philippa struck her steed smartly with the whip and controlled his resultant friskiness with admirable skill.

"Well, you know it's pleasanter," I said, wickedly. "Just think what a doleful world it would be if everybody were sensible."

Aunt Philippa looked at me out of the corner of her eye and disdained any skirmish of flippant epigram.

"So you want to get married?" she said. "You'd better wait till you're grown up."

"How old must a person be before she is grown up?" I asked gravely.

"Humph! That depends. Some are grown up when they're born, and others ain't grown up when they're eighty. That same Mrs. Roderick I was speaking of never grew up. She was as foolish when she was a hundred as when she was ten."

"Perhaps that's why she lived so long," I suggested. All thought of seeking sympathy in Aunt Philippa had vanished. I resolved I would not even mention Mark's name.

"Mebbe 'twas," admitted Aunt Philippa with a grim smile. "*I'd* rather live fifty sensible years than a hundred foolish ones."

Much to my relief, she made no further reference to my

affairs. As we rounded a curve in the road where two great over-arching elms met, a buggy wheeled by us, occupied by a young man in clerical costume. He had a pleasant, boyish face, and he touched his hat courteously. Aunt Philippa nodded very frostily and gave her horse a quite undeserved cut.

"There's a man you don't want to have much to do with," she said portentously. "He's a Methodist minister."

"Why, Auntie, the Methodists are a very nice denomination," I protested. "My stepmother is a Methodist, you know."

"No, I didn't know, but I'd believe anything of a stepmother. I've no use for Methodists or their ministers. This fellow just came last spring, and it's *my* opinion he smokes. And he thinks every girl who looks at him falls in love with him – as if a Methodist minister was any prize! Don't you take much notice of him, Ursula."

"I'll not be likely to have the chance," I said, with an amused smile.

"Oh, you'll see enough of him. He boards at Mrs. John Callman's, just across the road from us, and he's always out sunning himself on her verandah. Never studies, of course. Last Sunday they say he preached on the iron that floated. If he'd confine himself to the Bible and leave sensational subjects alone it would be better for him and his poor congregation, and so I told Mrs. John Callman to her face. I should think *she* would have had enough of his sex by this time. She married John Callman against her father's will, and he had delirious trembles for years. That's the men for you."

"They're not *all* like that, Aunt Philippa," I protested.

"Most of 'em are. See that house over there? Mrs. Jane Harrison lives there. Her husband took tantrums every few days or so and wouldn't get out of bed. She had to do all the barn work till he'd got over his spell. That's men for you. When he died, people writ her letters of condolence but *I* just sot down and writ her one of congratulation. There's the Presbyterian manse in the hollow. Mr. Bentwell's our minister. He's a good man and he'd be a rather nice one if he didn't think it was his duty to be a little miserable all the time. He won't let his wife wear a fashionable hat, and his daughter can't fix her hair the way she wants to. Even being a minister can't prevent a man from being a crank. Here's Ebenezer Milgrave coming. You take a good look at him. He used to be insane for years. He believed he was dead and used to rage at his wife because she wouldn't bury him. *I'd* a-done it."

Aunt Philippa looked so determinedly grim that I could almost see her with a spade in her hand. I laughed aloud at the picture summoned up.

"Yes, it's funny, but I guess his poor wife didn't find it very humorsome. He's been pretty sane for some years now, but you never can tell when he'll break out again. He's got a brother, Albert Milgrave, who's been married twice. They say he was courting his second wife while his first was dying. Let that be as it may, he used his first wife's wedding ring to marry the second. That's the men for you."

"Don't you know *any* good husbands, Aunt Philippa?" I asked desperately.

"Oh, yes, lots of 'em – over there," said Aunt Philippa sardonically, waving her whip in the direction of a little country graveyard on a distant hill.

"Yes, but *living* – walking about in the flesh?"

"Precious few. Now and again you'll come across a man whose wife won't put up with any nonsense and he *has* to be respectable. But the most of 'em are poor bargains – poor bargains."

"And are all the wives saints?" I persisted.

"Laws, no, but they're too good for the men," retorted Aunt Philippa, as she turned in at her own gate. Her house was close to the road and was painted such a vivid green that the landscape looked faded by contrast. Across the gable end of it was the legend, "Philippa's Farm," emblazoned in huge black letters two feet long. All its surroundings were very neat. On the kitchen doorstep a patchwork cat was making a grave toilet. The groundwork of the cat was white, and its spots were black, yellow, grey, and brown.

"There's Joseph," said Aunt Philippa. "I call him that because his coat is of many colours. But I ain't no lover of cats. They're too much like the men to suit me."

"Cats have always been supposed to be peculiarly feminine," I said, descending.

"'Twas a man that supposed it, then," retorted Aunt Philippa, beckoning to her hired boy. "Here, Jerry, put Prince away. Jerry's a good sort of boy," she confided to me as we went into the house. "I had Jim Spencer last summer and the only good thing about *him* was his appetite. I put up with him till harvest was in, and then one day my patience give out. He upsot a churnful of cream in the back yard – and was just as cool as a cowcumber over it – laughed and said it was good for the land. I told him I wasn't in the habit of fertilizing my back yard with cream. But that's the men for you. Come in. I'll have tea ready in no time. I sot the table before I left. There's lemon pie. Mrs. John Cantwell sent it over. I never make lemon pie myself. Ten years ago I took the prize for lemon pies at the county fair, and I've never made any since for fear I'd lose my reputation for them."

THE FIRST MONTH of my stay passed not unpleasantly. The summer weather was delightful, and the sea air was certainly splendid. Aunt Philippa's little farm ran right down to the shore, and I spent much of my time there. There were also several families of cousins to be visited in the farmhouses that dotted the pretty, seaward-sloping valley, and they came back to see me at "Philippa's Farm." I picked spruce gum and berries and ferns, and Aunt Philippa taught me to make butter. It was all very idyllic – or would have been if Mark had written. But Mark did not write. I supposed he must be very angry because I had run off to Prince Edward Island without so much as a note of goodbye. But I had been so sure he would understand!

Aunt Philippa never made any further reference to the reason Father had sent me to her, but she allowed no day to pass without holding up to me some horrible example of matrimonial infelicity. The number of unhappy wives who walked or drove past "Philippa's Farm" every afternoon, as we sat on the verandah, was truly pitiable.

We always sat on the verandah in the afternoon, when we were not visiting or being visited. I made a pretence of fancy work, and Aunt Philippa spun diligently on a little old-fashioned spinning-wheel that had been her grandmother's. She always sat before the wood stand which held her flowers, and the gorgeous blots of geranium blossom and big green leaves furnished a pretty background. She always wore her shapeless but clean print wrappers, and her iron-grey hair was always combed neatly down over her ears. Joseph sat between us, sleeping or purring. She spun so expertly that she could keep a close watch on the road as well, and I got the biography of every individual who went by. As for the poor young Methodist minister, who liked to read or walk on the verandah of our neighbour's house, Aunt Philippa never had a good word for him. I had met him once or twice socially and had liked him. I wanted to ask him to call but dared not – Aunt Philippa had vowed he should never enter her house.

"If I was dead and he came to my funeral I'd rise up and order him out," she said.

"I thought he made a very nice prayer at Mrs. Seaman's funeral the other day," I said.

"Oh, I've no doubt he can pray. I never heard anyone make more beautiful prayers than old Simon Kennedy down at the harbour, who was always drunk or hoping to be – and the drunker he was the better he prayed. It ain't no matter how well a man prays if his preaching isn't right. That Methodist man preaches a lot of things that ain't true, and what's worse they ain't sound doctrine. At least, that's what I've heard. I never was in a Methodist church, thank goodness."

"Don't you think Methodists go to heaven as well as Presbyterians, Aunt Philippa?" I asked gravely.

"That ain't for us to decide," said Aunt Philippa solemnly. "It's in higher hands than ours. But I ain't going to associate with them on *earth*, whatever I may have to do in heaven. The folks round here mostly don't make much difference and go to the Methodist church quite often. But *I* say if you are a Presbyterian, *be* a Presbyterian. Of course, if you ain't, it don't matter much what you do. As for that minister man, he has a grand-uncle who was sent to the penitentiary for embezzlement. I found out *that* much."

And evidently Aunt Philippa had taken an unholy joy in finding it out.

"I dare say some of our own ancestors deserved to go to the penitentiary, even if they never did," I remarked. "Who is that woman driving past, Aunt Philippa? She must have been very pretty once."

"She was – and that was all the good it did her. 'Favour is deceitful and beauty is vain,' Ursula. She was Sarah Pyatt and she married Fred Proctor. He was one of your wicked, fascinating men. After she married him he give up being fascinating but he kept on being wicked. *That's* the men for you. Her sister Flora weren't much luckier. *Her* man was that domineering she couldn't call her soul her own. Finally he couldn't get his own way over something and he just suicided by jumping into the well. A good riddance – but of course the well was spoiled. Flora could never abide the thought of using it again, poor thing. *That's* men for you.

"And there's that old Enoch Allan on his way to the station. He's ninety if he's a day. You can't kill some folks with a meat axe. His wife died twenty years ago. He'd been married when he was twenty so they'd lived together for fifty years. She was a faithful, hard-working creature and kept him out of the poorhouse, for he was a shiftless soul, not lazy, exactly, but just too fond of sitting. But he weren't grateful. She had a kind of bitter tongue and they did use to fight scandalous. O' course it was all his fault. Well, she died, and old Enoch and my father drove together to the graveyard. Old Enoch was awful quiet all the way there and back, but just afore they got home, he says solemnly to Father: 'You mayn't believe it, Henry, but this is the happiest day of my life.' *That's* men for you. His brother, Scotty Allan, was the meanest man ever lived in these parts. When his wife died she was buried with a little gold brooch in her collar unbeknownst to him. When he found it out he went one night to the graveyard and opened up the grave and the casket to get that brooch."

"Oh, Aunt Philippa, that is a horrible story," I cried, recoiling with a shiver over the gruesomeness of it.

"'Course it is, but what would you expect of a man?" retorted Aunt Philippa.

Somehow, her stories began to affect me in spite of myself. There were times when I felt very dreary. Perhaps Aunt Philippa was right. Perhaps men possessed neither truth nor constancy. Certainly Mark had forgotten me. I was ashamed of myself because this hurt me so much, but I could not help it. I grew pale and listless. Aunt Philippa sometimes peered at me sharply, but she held her peace. I was grateful for this.

BUT ONE DAY a letter did come from Mark. I dared not read it until I was safely in my own room. Then I opened it with trembling fingers.

The letter was a little stiff. Evidently Mark was feeling sore enough over things. He made no reference to our quarrel or to my sojourn in Prince Edward Island. He wrote that his firm was sending him to South Africa to take charge of their interests there. He would leave in three weeks' time and could not return for five years. If I still cared anything for him, would I meet him in Halifax, marry him, and go to South Africa with him? If I would not, he would understand that I had ceased to love him and that all was over between us.

That, boiled down, was the gist of Mark's letter. When I had read it I cast myself on the bed and wept out all the tears I had refused to let myself shed during my weeks of exile.

For I could not do what Mark asked – I *could not.* I couldn't run away to be married in that desolate, unbefriended fashion. It would be a disgrace. I would feel ashamed of it all my life and be unhappy over it. I thought that Mark was rather unreasonable. He knew what my feelings about runaway marriages were. And was it absolutely necessary for him to go to South Africa? Of course his father was behind it somewhere, but surely he could have got out of it if he had really tried.

Well, if he went to South Africa he must go alone. But my heart would break.

I cried the whole afternoon, cowering among my pillows. I never wanted to go out of that room again. I never wanted to see anybody again. I hated the thought of facing Aunt Philippa with her cold eyes and her miserable stories that seemed to strip life of all beauty and love of all reality. I could hear her scornful, "That's the men for you," if she heard what was in Mark's letter.

"What is the matter, Ursula?"

Aunt Philippa was standing by my bed. I was too abject to resent her coming in without knocking.

"Nothing," I said spiritlessly.

"If you've been crying for three mortal hours over nothing you want a good spanking and you'll get it," observed Aunt Philippa placidly, sitting down on my trunk. "Get right up off that bed this minute and tell me what the trouble is. I'm bound to know, for I'm in your father's place at present."

"There, then!" I flung her Mark's letter. There wasn't anything in it that it was sacrilege to let another person see. That was one reason why I had been crying.

Aunt Philippa read it over twice. Then she folded it up deliberately and put it back in the envelope.

"What are you going to do?" she asked in a matter-of-fact tone.

"I'm not going to run away to be married," I answered sullenly.

"Well, no, I wouldn't advise you to," said Aunt Philippa reflectively. "It's a kind of low-down thing to do, though there's been a terrible lot of romantic nonsense talked and writ about eloping. It may be a painful necessity sometimes, but it ain't in this case. You write to your young man and tell him to come here and be married respectable under my roof, same as a Goodwin ought to."

I sat up and stared at Aunt Philippa. I was so amazed that it is useless to try to express my amazement.

"Aunt – Philippa," I gasped. "I thought – I thought –"

"You thought I was a hard old customer, and so I am," said Aunt Philippa. "But I don't take my opinions from your father nor anybody else. It didn't prejudice me any against your young man that your father didn't like him. I knew your father of old. I have some other friends in Montreal and I writ to them and asked them what he was like. From what they said I judged he was decent enough as men go. You're too young to be married, but if you let him go off to South Africa he'll slip through your fingers for sure, and I s'pose you're like some of the rest of us – nobody'll do you but the one. So tell him to come here and be married."

"I don't see how I can," I gasped. "I can't get ready to be married in three weeks. I can't –"

"I should think you have enough clothes in that trunk to do you for a spell," said Aunt Philippa sarcastically. "You've more than my mother ever had in all her life. We'll get you a wedding dress of some kind. You can get it made in Charlottetown, if country dressmakers aren't good enough for you, and I'll bake you a wedding cake that'll taste as good as anything you could get in Montreal, even if it won't look so stylish."

"What will Father say?" I questioned.

"Lots o' things," conceded Aunt Philippa grimly. "But I don't see as it matters when neither you nor me'll be there to have our feelings hurt. I'll write a few things to your father. He hasn't got much sense. He ought to be thankful to get a decent young man for his son-in-law in a world where 'most every man is a wolf in sheep's clothing. But that's the men for you."

And that was Aunt Philippa for you. For the next three weeks she was a blissfully excited, busy woman. I was allowed to choose the material and fashion of my wedding suit and hat myself, but almost everything else was settled by Aunt Philippa. I didn't mind; it was a relief to be rid of all responsibility; I did protest when she declared her intention of having a big wedding and asking all the cousins and semi-cousins on the island, but Aunt Philippa swept my objections lightly aside.

"I'm bound to have one good wedding in this house," she said. "Not likely I'll ever have another chance."

She found time amid all the baking and concocting to warn me frequently not to take it too much to heart if Mark failed to come after all.

"I know a man who jilted a girl on her wedding day. That's the men for you. It's best to be prepared."

But Mark did come, getting there the evening before our wedding day. And then a severe blow fell on Aunt Philippa. Word came from the manse that Mr. Bentwell had been suddenly summoned to Nova Scotia to his mother's deathbed; he had started that night.

"That's the men for you," said Aunt Philippa bitterly.

"Never can depend on one of them, not even on a minister. What's to be done now?"

"Get another minister," said Mark easily.

"Where'll you get him?" demanded Aunt Philippa. "The minister at Cliftonville is away on his vacation, and Mercer is vacant, and that leaves none nearer than town. It won't do to depend on a town minister being able to come. No, there's no help for it. You'll have to have that Methodist man."

Aunt Philippa's tone was tragic. Plainly she thought the ceremony would scarcely be legal if that Methodist man married us. But neither Mark nor I cared. We were too happy to be disturbed by any such trifles.

The young Methodist minister married us the next day in the presence of many beaming guests. Aunt Philippa, splendid in black silk and point-lace collar, neither of which lost a whit of dignity or lustre by being made ten years before, was composure itself while the ceremony was going on. But no sooner had the minister pronounced us man and wife than she spoke up.

"Now that's over I want someone to go right out and put out the fire on the kitchen roof. It's been on fire for the last ten minutes."

Minister and bridegroom headed the emergency brigade, and Aunt Philippa pumped the water for them. In a short time the fire was out, all was safe, and we were receiving our deferred congratulations.

"Now, young man," said Aunt Philippa solemnly as she shook hands with Mark, "don't you ever try to get out of this, even if a Methodist minister did marry you."

She insisted on driving us to the train and said goodbye to us as we stood on the car steps. She had caught more of the shower of rice than I had, and as the day was hot and sunny she had tied over her head, atop of that festal silk dress, a huge, home-made, untrimmed straw hat. But she did not look ridiculous. There was a certain dignity about Aunt Philippa in any costume and under any circumstance.

"Aunt Philippa," I said, "tell me this: why have you helped me to be married?"

The train began to move.

"I refused once to run away myself, and I've repented it ever since." Then, as the train gathered speed and the distance between us widened, she shouted after us, "But I s'pose if I had run away I'd have repented of that too."

A Dinner of Herbs

UT – but," said Robin Lyle blankly, "that is impossible, Myra."

In the bright lexicon of Mrs. George Lyle there was no such word as impossible.

"Not at all," she said briskly. "In fact, it's necessary. The twins must have a room to themselves now. The boys will have Grandma's room. So of course Gladys must room with you. That big west room is large enough for a dozen, I'm sure."

There was a note of dissatisfaction in Myra Lyle's voice. She had always been secretly resentful that Robin should have that big sunny room – the only room with a fireplace. Myra wanted it for a guest-room. But as long as Grandma Lyle lived one could do nothing about it. And in some matters George was stubborn, though generally his wife led him round by the ear.

Robin continued to look blank. Yet she said nothing more. She had not lived sixteen years under the same roof with Myra Lyle without learning the futility of saying anything – even when her mother was alive. And now that her mother was dead, there would be no check on Myra. George simply did not count – George who had always thought, thought still, and would continue to think, that Robin must be "brought up."

Her silence and her blankness worried Myra a bit. Myra could not understand silence – could not understand anyone who did not think at the top of her voice and empty her feelings out to the dregs. Of course, Robin had always been a sly, secretive thing.

"Why should you mind sharing your room with Gladys?" she demanded, answering Robin's silence. "I'd think you'd *like* to have a young life so near you to keep you from growing old."

"I don't mind growing old if I can be left to do it in peace," said Robin. "I'm sure I won't like rooming with a young girl."

"Well, it won't be for long. I think Irving Keyes will see to that."

There was a smirk on Myra's face which had the same effect on Robin that a dig in the ribs with Myra's fat elbow would have had. In fact, she could not endure it. She turned and went out of the room, in silence. Myra sighed – she had "put up" with that for sixteen years. Then Myra smiled. Irving Keyes! And a widower always meant business. Myra went back to her sewing. Things were working out very nicely. Grandma was out of the way at last, and Robin would soon be off their hands. A good match too – one the clan would approve of! George had been foolish to think Robin had a notion of Michael Stanislaws – Michael, who was poor and hadn't even the decency to be ashamed of it. Shell-shocked in the war, with a lean brown face scarred by shrapnel, and a leg that wasn't much use, he was just baching it over at Owl's Roost and pottering round his show dahlias, with two black cats forever at his heels. No, no, Robin was no fool. But she must be told not to dilly-dally with her good fortune. Before her mother's death there had been some talk of Irving Keyes's interest in Blanche Foster, a handsome girl much younger than Robin. Myra found it hard to believe that anyone could prefer pale, old-maidish Robin to her. Yet, as Irving Keyes seemed to be blessedly inclined that way, Robin must be made to understand that she must not let him slip through her fingers – again. She would never have such another chance. A well-to-do merchant with the most expensive car in the village and a house with more ornamentation on it than any house in the country! Myra sighed and wondered why fate had given her only a farmer. She felt she would have shone as a general merchant's wife.

"As soon as Robin is married," she decided, "I'll give Gladys the guest-room and have the west room done over."

ROBIN WENT TO HER ROOM – the only spot on earth she had ever been able to call her own. And, as always when she went into it, the peace and dignity and beauty of it seemed to envelop her like a charm. She was in a different world – a world where George and Myra could not quarrel or the hired girl be impertinent to her; and the everlasting noise and racket of the household died away at its threshold like the spent wave of a troubled sea. For years all that had supported her through the drudgery of days spent waiting on a querulous invalid was the certainty of finding herself alone in her dear room at night where dreams gave some mysterious strength for another day.

The north window looked down on leagues of rippled sea and distant, misty, fairy-like coasts. Between it and the sand-dunes was only a dwindling grove of ragged old spruces.

The west window looked out on Owl's Roost, with its orchard and garden, where First and Second Peter prowled darkly, and Michael himself played his violin at hours when all decent people should be in bed. Sometimes, too, he ate his slender meals in the orchard, under an enormous apple tree, never dreaming that Robin Lyle was watching him from her window and wishing shamelessly that she might play "Thou" to his crust of bread and jug of milk. Nor was the book of verse wanting. Michael read as he ate, propping his book up against the jug.

And now all this would be taken from her. She knew exactly what rooming with Gladys and her shrieking chums would mean. No more dreaming; no more shadowy hours of listening to Michael's stormy music in the orchard; no more early dawns watching the silent mysterious ships drift by the dunes to the harbour; never again alone with the night.

No, she could not endure it. Even sleek, prosperous Irving Keyes would be better than that.

"Life isn't fair," said Robin drearily, as if there was any use in saying it.

She went to the glass and looked at herself. She looked at her straight, black, bobbed hair, dark blue eyes and white, heart-shaped face; at her wide mouth quirked up at the corners so that she always seemed to be laughing even when very sad. And she thought of Blanche Foster's red-gold hair and flashing black eyes and brilliant complexion. Blanche Foster, who had always made Robin feel old and dowdy and silly. It was amazing that Irving Keyes didn't prefer her, but since he didn't . . .

Robin shivered a little and sat down by the west window in the moonlight. The window was open, and the faint, cold, sweet perfumes of night drifted in – blent with the whiff of Michael Stanislaws's pipe, neither faint nor sweet, but very alluring. Once, when she was eighteen, she had had a fleeting fancy for Irving Keyes – and he knew it. Even yet he was attractive – until he spoke. But his funny vulgar stories and his great haw-haws! And his love for practical jokes! He still thought it a joke to stick out his foot and trip somebody up. And he still thought it wit to call eggs cackleberries.

Irving Keyes had been heard to boast that he had got everything he wanted in life. And now he wanted Robin Lyle. Robin thought he would get that too, despite his roars of laughter and the jigarees on his house.

What else was there for her? Arnold Clive? No! She shivered again. Austere, religious Arnold with the face of a fanatic: high, narrow brow, deep-set intolerant eyes, merciless mouth – quite out of the question! And, after all, she liked Irving very well.

She looked over at Owl's Roost. What a nice, gentle little old house it was; a nice lazy old house – a house that had folded its hands and said, "I will rest." It had none of the Lyle efficiency and up-to-dateness about it, with a sly little eyebrow window above the porch roof and the magic of trees around it. She loved the trees around Owl's Roost. There were no trees around George's house. Myra thought shade unsanitary.

Michael was smoking his pipe at the fence with an orchard full of mysterious moonlit delights behind him. Robin wished she could go down and talk with him. She had sometimes talked with him over the fence. Not often, and yet she felt curiously well acquainted with him. They had laughed together the first time they had talked, and when two people have laughed – really laughed – together they are good friends for life.

Though Michael did not laugh much. If anything, he was bitter. But there was something stimulating and pungent about his bitterness – like choke-cherries. They puckered your mouth horribly, but still you hankered for them.

"I wonder what he is thinking of," thought Robin.

She *knew* she only thought it. Yet a voice drifted up to her from the orchard.

"I'm thinking how very silvery that dark cloud must be on the moon side," said the voice. "Come down here and help me watch it leaving the moon. It's as good as an eclipse."

Robin flew downstairs, out of the side door and along the brick walk, worn by many feet. Michael was hanging over the fence. First Peter sat hunched up beside him, and Second Peter smoothed about his shoulder. First Peter always let Robin stroke him, but Second Peter swore at her. Second Peter was not to be hoodwinked.

Robin stood beside Michael on the other side of the fence, where the moonlight would lie white as snow on the flagged walk when the cloud passed. She had never been through the fence. There was no gate between the Lyle yard and the old orchard, lying fragrant and velvety under the enchantment of night.

They stood there together in a wonderful silence until the cloud had passed.

"'He who has seen the full moon break forth from behind a dark cloud at night, has been present like an archangel at the creation of light and of the world,'" quoted Michael, whacking his pipe on the fence and putting it in his pocket. "Wasn't it worth watching, Miss Lyle?"

If there was one thing she hated more than another, it was having Michael call her "Miss Lyle." She hated it so much that she answered "Yes," stiffly and unenthusiastically.

"It's impossible to avoid the conclusion that something is bothering you," said Michael. "Tell First Peter about it and I'll listen in."

A perfectly crazy impulse mastered Robin. She *would* tell him. She had to tell somebody.

"I can't make up my mind which of two men to marry," she said bluntly.

Michael was silent for an appreciable space. All the sounds audible were First Peter purring and a dog taking the countryside into his confidence two farms away. His silence got on Robin's nerves.

"That wasn't quite true," she said crossly. "There *are* two – but there's only one I could really consider possible. And the trouble is I *don't* want to marry him – or anyone," she added hastily, telling a second tarradiddle.

"Then why marry him?" said Michael. "Why marry at all if you don't want to, in this day of woman's emancipation?"

"The trouble is – I'm not emancipated," sighed Robin, wishing that First Peter would stop purring. It was outrageous that a cat should be so blatantly happy. Though why shouldn't he be happy? Couldn't he sit on Michael's shoulder and snuggle his nose against Michael's face? Wasn't he doing it now, darn him! Yet she was still talking on. "I'm twenty years behind the times. I'm thirty-three and I'm not trained to do anything. I've no special gift. I can't sew or teach or pound a typewriter. All I can do, or want to do, is keep house. And I *must* marry – or room with Gladys."

"Do you think Irving Keyes would be a more agreeable room-mate?" said Michael sarcastically – though she had not said anything about Irving Keyes.

"Well, he won't plaster my dressing table with powder – or raise Cain when he can't find his hairpins – or yell to Baal if he has chilblains – or look in the mirror the same time I do – *purposely*," said Robin defiantly.

"I think I see what you're up against," said Michael, beginning to fill his pipe again.

"You don't – not fully – a *man* couldn't," snapped Robin. "Gladys will talk me to death about her beaus. Gladys thinks there's no fun in having a beau unless you can tell everybody about him and what he said and what he did. She'll laugh at my funny old pictures with big sleeves and hats high on the head. She'll come in and wake me up in the wee sma's. She'll insist on having the most awful silver pig with a blue velvet pincushion on his back on my table. She'll bring her rampageous school chums in and chitter-chatter for hours. And everything will be either wonderful or priceless. I'll never be alone any more," concluded Robin pathetically.

"*That* gets me," said Michael. "And the alternative is Irving Keyes. A handsome fellow with gobs of money. Why don't you like him?"

"I do. But I don't feel like marrying him, for several reasons."

"For instance . . ."

"He likes bread thick, and I like it thin," said Robin flippantly. She felt she had been absurd in telling Michael as much as she had.

"Every proper man likes bread thick. I've no sympathy with you there."

"Our taste in jokes is entirely different."

"Ah, *that's* serious," said Michael, not sounding serious.

"And . . ." Robin looked at another cloud that was creeping over the moon. "I – I want someone else."

"Oh!" Second Peter snarled, as if he had been pushed aside with a foot.

"He's the only man in the world for me," said Robin, looking straight at Michael.

"That's a large order out of approximately five hundred million men," said Michael drily.

He began to smoke insolently. The cloud was over the moon, and the world was dark. Robin felt cold and old and silly and empty.

"I must go in," she said.

"Wait a sec." Michael was rummaging in his pocket. "Here's something for your rose-jar."

He handed her over a paper bag full of dried rose-leaves.

"All I can give any woman now – withered rose-leaves," he said lightly. "Irving's a good fellow. Perhaps you can teach him to laugh in the right place. I'd have a try."

ROBIN WENT AWAY for two weeks to visit a school chum two years older than herself whose daughter was engaged. She had not been away for a visit for ten years. When she came back, Michael asked her (still over the fence) if good wishes were in order.

"Not yet," said Robin airily. She thought Michael looked tired and a bit old.

"I've promised to give him his answer today. *Write* it to him. I couldn't say 'yes' face to face."

"But I'm quite sure 'yes' is the best thing to say," said Michael, stooping to tickle Second Peter's ear. Second Peter snarled. You *couldn't* hoodwink Second Peter.

"Of course it is," said Robin piteously. "But the trouble is – I don't *want* to say it – Michael."

Somehow their eyes met. Eyes can say so much in just a second. At least Robin's could. Michael's didn't say anything. She realized that he had looked into her heart, but that she had not even had a peep into his.

"I'm horribly poor," said Michael slowly.

"But laughter would always be a guest in our house," said Robin.

"I always have First Peter sleeping on the foot of the bed."

"Why not Second Peter too?"

"Everything in my house is chipped or mended or torn."

"We wouldn't be afraid to use it, then."

"I've got a temper, and shell-shock didn't improve it. We'd fight often."

"Husbands and wives have a right to fight now and then, haven't they?"

"Getting up before breakfast and working between meals isn't supposed to be to my liking."

"After thirty-three years of George's efficiency, a lazy man would be nice for a change."

"I'm inclined to be a vegetarian."

"'Better a dinner of herbs,'" quoted Robin.

"All the ready cash I have in the world just at present is ten dollars."

"Enough for a licence and a wedding ring," said Robin brazenly.

"Let's take a chance at it then," said Michael, looking at First Peter.

Robin laughed under her breath. She sobbed the next minute. She flung out her hands as if to push Michael and Peter and the fence a thousand miles away.

"Oh, my dear – my dear, how funny you are," she said. "Why, I wouldn't marry you if you were the last one of the five hundred million left alive in the world."

Michael's face was expressionless. He looked past her at Second Peter on an apple-tree bough, still refusing to be hoodwinked.

"Sorry," he said. "I thought you would like the idea. My mistake."

George Lyle scowled at Robin when she went in.

"Don't make a fool of yourself over Michael Stanislaws," he said bluntly.

"But isn't that just what I've done?" said Robin.

"What do you mean?"

"I've just refused to marry him."

"Thank heaven you'd enough sense for that," said relieved George.

There were five doors on the way to her room and Robin banged them all. Oh, so he pitied her! She had badgered him into asking her to marry him out of pity. Oh, she'd show him. She flew to her table – she would write Irving Keyes his answer on the spot.

"Cat, are you laughing?" Michael was saying furiously to Second Peter.

Robin went down to the mailbox ostentatiously after dinner to mail her letter. Michael was tying up his dahlias as she passed and waved his hand airily at her. Robin had to wave back because she hadn't been able to make up her mind as yet whether to hate or ignore him. She waved with the hand that held Irving Keyes's letter.

Michael had gone from the garden when she came back. He was sitting on his shaky verandah talking to a man who had presumably come in the smart green car parked in the lane. There was a pile of shabby old books on the chair between them. She could hear Michael laughing. She went up to her room – hers for one day more only – and sat down by the west window. The mailbox was hidden from her view by the wild cherry at the gate, but presently the postman's motor wheeled by. Robin shivered. Her letter was gone – irrevocably. At once a panic horror of her future seized her. Why had she? Oh, why had she?

At sunset Michael came to the fence and called her. Robin, deciding that you should at least be civil to a rejected suitor, asked him from her window what he wanted.

"I've a sin on my conscience. Perhaps worse – a mistake," Michael called back. "Come down and let me confess."

Robin told herself she was not interested in Michael's sins, but she went down. He was leaning on the fence and his cap was pulled down so far that she couldn't see his eyes.

"Do you think Irving Keyes has your letter by now?" he said impertinently.

"He should have."

"Well, he hasn't. That letter is in ashes in my kitchen stove. I went down and took it out of the mailbox before the postman came. You can put me in the pen for that, I believe."

Robin looked at Second Peter, who had the air of making up his mind to the inevitable.

"Why did you do that?"

"I found it was simply impossible to let you marry another man. Why did you refuse my heart and hand and my few insignificant worldly goods this morning?"

"I wasn't going to be married out of pity."

"Pity! Do you suppose I've committed a felony – or is it only a misdemeanour – out of pity? I've loved you ever since that first day we talked over the fence. But I'm so poor – and lame – and ugly."

"You're not ugly and not very lame and I don't care how poor you are," said Robin so shamelessly that Second Peter blushed for her.

Michael leaned over the fence and took her hand.

"I found out this afternoon that my old edition of *The Pilgrim's Progress* is worth a thousand dollars. Shall we put the money in the bank for a rainy day or run over to Europe for our honeymoon in places I know over there? There's a village in the Apennines – 'the cloudy Apennines' . . ."

"Let us go to Europe," said Robin recklessly. "Umbrellas have been invented since that proverb was."

Second Peter was so disgusted at what followed that he stalked away bristling. But he had always known it – always expected it. You couldn't hoodwink Second Peter.

"Did you read that letter?" Robin asked, before she went in to have it out with George and Myra.

"Of course not," said Michael indignantly. "I may be a thief, but I'm not a sneak."

"It's a pity you didn't," said Robin coolly, "because if you had you'd have seen that I refused him."

Jessamine

HEN the vegetable-man knocked, Jessamine went to the door wearily. She felt quite well acquainted with him. He had been coming all the spring, and his cheery greeting always left a pleasant afterglow behind him. But it was not the vegetable-man, after all – at least, not the right one. This one was considerably younger. He was tall and sunburned, with a ruddy, smiling face, and keen, pleasant blue eyes; and he had a spray of honeysuckle pinned on his coat.

"Want any garden stuff this morning?"

Jessamine shook her head. "We always get ours from Mr. Bell. This is his day to come."

"Well, I guess you won't see Mr. Bell for a spell. He fell off a loft out at his place yesterday and broke his leg. I'm his nephew, and I'm going to fill his place till he gets 'round again."

"Oh, I'm so sorry – for Mr. Bell, I mean. Have you any green peas?"

"Yes, heaps of them. I'll bring them in. Anything else?"

"Not today," said Jessamine, with a wistful glance at the honeysuckle.

Mr. Bell, junior, saw it. In an instant the honeysuckle was unpinned and handed to her. "If you like posies, you're welcome to this. I guess you're fond of flowers," he added, as he noted the flash of delight that passed over her pale face.

"Yes, indeed; they put me so in mind of home – of the country. Oh, how sweet this is!"

"You're country-bred, then? Been in the city long?"

"Since last fall. I was born and brought up in the country. I wish I was back. I can't get over being homesick. This honeysuckle seems to bring it right back. We had honeysuckles around our porch at home."

"You don't like the city, then?"

"Oh, no. I sometimes feel as if I should smother here. I shall never feel at home, I am afraid."

"Where did you live before you came here?"

"Up at Middleton. It was an old-fashioned place, but so pretty – our house was covered with vines, and there were big trees all about it, and great green fields beyond. But I don't know what makes me tell you this. I forgot I was talking to a stranger."

"Pretty little woman," soliloquized Andrew Bell, as he drove away. "She doesn't look happy, though. I suppose she's married some city chap and has to live in town. I guess it don't agree with her. Her eyes had a real hungry look in them over that honeysuckle. She seemed near about crying when she talked of the country."

Jessamine felt more like crying than ever when she went back to her work. Her head ached and she was very tired. The tiny kitchen was hot and stifling. How she longed for the great, roomy kitchen in her old home, with its spotless floors and floods of sunshine streaming in through the maples outside. There was room to live and breathe there; and from the door one looked out over green wind-rippled meadows, under a glorious arch of pure blue sky, away to the purple hills in the distance.

JESSAMINE STACY had always lived in the country. When her sister died and the old home had to go, Jessamine could only accept the shelter offered by her brother, John Stacy, who did business in the city.

Of her stylish sister-in-law Jessamine was absolutely in awe. At first Mrs. John was by no means pleased at the necessity of taking a country sister into her family circle. But one day, when the servant girl took a tantrum and left, Mrs. John found it very convenient to have in the house a person who could step into Eliza's place as promptly and efficiently as Jessamine could.

Indeed, she found it so convenient that Eliza never had a successor. Jessamine found herself in the position of maid-of-all-work and kitchen drudge for board and clothes.

She never complained, but she grew thinner and paler as the winter went by. She had worked as hard on the farm, but it was the close confinement and weary routine that told on her. Mrs. John was exacting and querulous. John was absorbed in his business worries and had no time to waste on his sister. Now, when the summer had come, her homesickness was almost unbearable.

The next day Mr. Bell came he handed her a big bunch of sweet-brier roses.

"Here you are," he said heartily. "I took the liberty to bring you these today, seeing you're so fond of posies. The country roads are pink with them now. Why don't you get your husband to bring you out for a drive some day? You'd be as welcome as a lark at my farm."

"I will when he comes along, but I haven't seen him yet."

Mr. Bell gave a prolonged whistle. "Excuse me. I thought you were Mrs. Something-or-other for sure. Aren't you mistress here?"

"Oh, no. My brother's wife is the mistress here. I'm only Jessamine."

She laughed again. She was holding the roses against her face, and her eyes sparkled over them roguishly. The vegetable-man looked at her admiringly.

"You're a country rose yourself, miss, and you ought to be blooming out in the fields, instead of wilting in here."

"I wish I was. Thank you so much for the roses, Mr. – Mr. –"

"Bell – Andrew Bell, that's my name. I live out at Pine Pastures. We're all Bells out there – can't throw a stone without hitting one. Glad you like the roses."

After that the vegetable-man brought Jessamine a bouquet every trip. Now it was a big bunch of field-daisies or golden buttercups, now a green glory of spicy ferns, now a cluster of old-fashioned garden flowers.

"They keep life in me," Jessamine told him.

They were great friends by this time. True, she knew little about him but she felt instinctively that he was manly and kind-hearted.

One day when he came Jessamine met him almost gleefully. "No, nothing today. There is no dinner to cook."

"You don't say. Where are the folks?"

"Gone on an excursion. They won't be back until tonight."

"They won't? Well, I'll tell you what to do. You get ready, and when I'm through my rounds we'll go for a drive up the country."

"Oh, Mr. Bell! But won't it be too much bother for you?"

"Well, I reckon not! You want an excursion as well as other folks, and you shall have it."

"Oh, thank you so much. Yes, I'll be ready. You don't know how much it means to me."

"Poor little creature," said Mr. Bell, as he drove away. "It's downright cruelty, that's what it is, to keep her penned up like that. You might as well coop up a lark in a hen-house and expect it to thrive and sing. I'd like to give that brother of hers a piece of my mind."

When he lifted her up to the high seat of his express wagon that afternoon he said, "Now, I want you to do something. Just shut your eyes and don't open them again until I tell you to."

Jessamine laughed and obeyed. Finally she heard him say, "Look."

Jessamine opened her eyes with a little cry. They were on a remote country road, cool and dim and quiet, in the very heart of the beech woods. Long banners of light fell athwart the grey boles. Along the roadsides grew sheets of feathery ferns. Above the sky was gloriously blue. The air was sweet with the wild woodsy smell of the forest.

Jessamine lifted and clasped her hands in rapture. "Oh, how lovely!"

"Do you know where we're going?" said Mr. Bell delightedly. "Out to my farm at Pine Pastures. My aunt keeps house for me, and she'll be real glad to see you. You're just going to have a real good time this afternoon."

They had a delightful drive to begin with, and presently Mr. Bell turned into a wide lane.

"This is Cloverside Farm. I'm proud of it, I'll admit. There isn't a finer place in the county. What do you think of it?"

"Oh, it is lovely – it is like home. Look at those great fields. I'd like to go and lie down in that clover."

Mr. Bell lifted her from the wagon and marched her up a flowery garden path. "You shall do it, and everything else you want to. Here, Aunt, this is the young lady I spoke of. Make her at home while I tend to the horses."

Miss Bell was a pleasant-faced woman with silver hair and kind blue eyes. She took Jessamine's hand in a friendly fashion.

"Come in, dear. You're welcome as a June rose."

When Mr. Bell returned, he found Jessamine standing on the porch with her hands full of honeysuckle and her cheeks pink with excitement.

"I declare, you've got roses already," he exclaimed. "If they'd only stay now, and not bleach out again. What's first now?"

"Oh, I don't know. There are so many things I want to do. Those flowers in the garden are calling me – and I want to go down to that hollow and pick buttercups – and I want to stay right here and look at things."

Mr. Bell laughed. "Come with me to the pasture and see my Jersey calves. They're something worth seeing. Come, Aunt. This way, Miss Stacy."

He led the way down the lane, the two women following

together. Jessamine thought she must be in a pleasant dream. The whole afternoon was a feast of delight to her starved heart. When sunset came she sat down, tired out, but radiant, on the porch steps. Her hat had slipped back and her hair was curling around her face. Her dark eyes were aglow; the roses still bloomed in her cheeks.

Mr. Bell looked at her admiringly. "If a man could see that pretty sight every night!" he thought. "And, Great Scott, why can't he? What's to prevent, I'd like to know?"

When the moon rose, Mr. Bell brought his team around and they drove back through the clear night, past the wonderful stillness of the great beech woods and the wide fields. The farmer looked sideways at his companion.

"The little thing wants to be petted and looked after," he thought. "She's just pining away for home and love. And why can't she have it? She's dying by inches in that hole back in town."

Jessamine, quite unsuspecting the farmer's meditations, was living over again in fancy the joys of the afternoon: the ramble in the pasture, the drink of water from the spring under the hillside pines, the bountiful, old-fashioned country supper in the vine-shaded dining-room, the cup of new milk in the dairy at sunset, and all the glory of skies and meadows and trees. How could she go back to her cage again?

THE NEXT WEEK Mr. Bell, senior, resumed his visits, and the young farmer came no more to the side door of No. 49. Jessamine missed him greatly. Mr. Bell, senior, never brought her clover or honeysuckle.

But one day his nephew suddenly reappeared. Jessamine opened the door for him, and her face lighted up, but Mr. Bell saw that she had been crying.

"Did you think I had forgotten you?" he asked. "Not a bit of it. Harvest was on and I couldn't get clear before. I've come to ask you when you intend to take another drive to

Cloverside Farm. What have you been up to? You look as if you'd been working too hard."

"I – I – haven't felt very well. I'm glad you came today, Mr. Bell. Perhaps I shall not see you again, and I wanted to say goodbye and thank you for all your kindness."

"Goodbye? Why, where are you going?"

"My brother went west a week ago," faltered Jessamine. She could not bring herself to tell the clear-eyed farmer that John Stacy had failed and had been obliged to start for the west without saying goodbye to his creditors. "His wife and I – are going too – next week."

"Oh, Jessamine," exclaimed Mr. Bell in despair, "don't go – you mustn't. I want you at Cloverside Farm. I came today on purpose to ask you. I love you and I'll make you happy if you'll marry me. What do you say, Jessamine?"

Jessamine, by way of answer, sat down on the nearest chair and began to cry.

"Oh, don't," said the wooer in distress. "I didn't want to make you feel bad. If you don't like the idea, I won't mention it again."

"Oh, it isn't that – but I – I thought nobody cared what became of me. You are so kind – I'm afraid I'd only be a bother to you . . ."

"I'll risk that. You shall have a happy home, little girl. Will you come to it?"

"Ye-e-e-s." It was very indistinct and faltering, but Mr. Bell heard it and considered it a most eloquent answer.

Mrs. John fumed and sulked and chose to consider herself hoodwinked and injured. But Mr. Bell was a resolute man, and a few days later he came for the last time to No. 49 and took his bride away with him.

As they drove through the beech woods he put his arm tenderly around the shy, smiling little woman beside him and said, "You'll never be sorry for this, my dear."

And she never was.

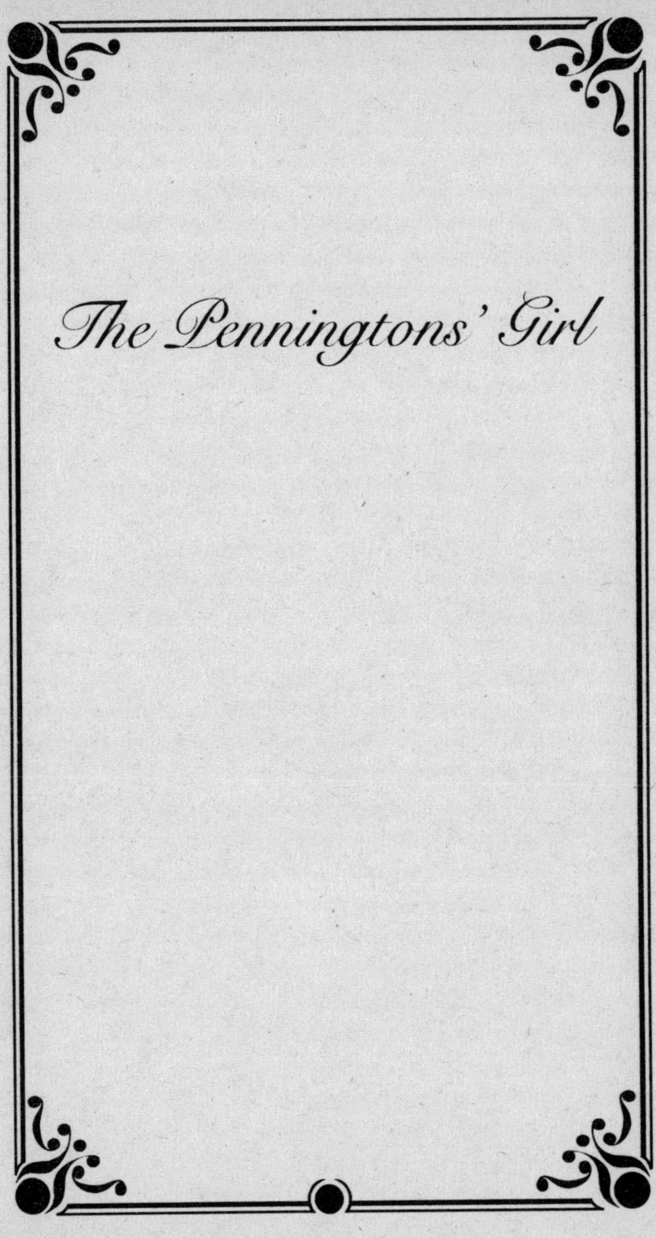

The Penningtons' Girl

INSLOW had been fishing – or pretending to – all the morning, and he was desperately thirsty. He boarded with the Beckwiths on the Riverside East Shore, but he was nearer Riverside West, and he knew the Penningtons well. He had often been there for bait and milk and had listened times out of mind to Mrs. Pennington's dismal tales of her tribulations with hired girls. She never could get along with them, and they left, on an average, after a fortnight's trial. She was on the lookout for one now, he knew, and would likely be cross, but he thought she would give him a drink.

He rowed his skiff into the shore and tied it to a fir that hung out from the bank. A winding little footpath led up to the Pennington farmhouse, which crested the hill about three hundred yards from the shore. Winslow made for the kitchen door and came face to face with a girl carrying a pail of water – Mrs. Pennington's latest thing in hired girls, of course.

Winslow's first bewildered thought was "What a goddess!" and he wondered, as he politely asked for a drink, where on earth Mrs. Pennington had picked her up. She handed him a shining dipper half full and stood, pail in hand, while he drank it.

She was rather tall, and wore a somewhat limp, faded print gown, and a big sunhat, beneath which a glossy knot of chestnut showed itself. Her skin was very fair, somewhat freckled, and her mouth was delicious. As for her eyes, they were grey, but beyond that simply defied description.

"Will you have some more?" she asked in a soft, drawling voice.

"No, thank you. That was delicious. Is Mrs. Pennington home?"

"No. She has gone away for the day."

"Well, I suppose I can sit down here and rest a while. You've no serious objections, have you?"

"Oh, no."

She carried her pail into the kitchen and came out again presently with a knife and a pan of apples. Sitting down on a bench under the poplars she proceeded to peel them with a disregard of his presence that piqued Winslow, who was not used to being ignored in this fashion. Besides, as a general rule, he had been quite good friends with Mrs. Pennington's hired girls. She had had three strapping damsels during his sojourn in Riverside, and he used to sit on this very doorstep and chaff them. They had all been saucy and talkative. This girl was evidently a new species.

"Do you think you'll get along with Mrs. Pennington?" he asked finally. "As a rule she fights with her help, although she is a most estimable woman."

The girl smiled quite broadly.

"I guess p'r'aps she's rather hard to suit," was the answer, "but I like her pretty well so far. I think we'll get along with each other. If we don't I can leave – like the others did."

"What is your name?"

"Nelly Ray."

"Well, Nelly, I hope you'll be able to keep your place. Let me give you a bit of friendly advice. Don't let the cats get into the pantry. That is what Mrs. Pennington has quarrelled with nearly every one of her girls about."

"It is quite a bother to keep them out, ain't it?" said Nelly calmly. "There's dozens of cats about the place. What on earth makes them keep so many?"

"Mr. Pennington has a mania for cats. He and Mrs. Pennington have a standing disagreement about it. The last girl left here because she couldn't stand the cats; they affected her nerves, she said. I hope you don't mind them."

"Oh, no; I kind of like cats. I've been tryin' to count them. Has anyone ever done that?"

"Not that I know of. I tried but I had to give up in despair – never could tell when I was counting the same cat over again. Look at that black goblin sunning himself on the woodpile. I say, Nelly, you're not going, are you?"

"I must. It's time to get dinner. Mr. Pennington will be in from the fields soon."

The next minute he heard her stepping briskly about the kitchen, shooing out intruding cats, and humming a darky air to herself. He went reluctantly back to the shore and rowed across the river in a brown study.

I don't know whether Winslow was afflicted with chronic thirst or not, or whether the East side water wasn't so good as that of the West side; but I do know that he fairly haunted the Pennington farmhouse after that. Mrs. Pennington was home the next time he went, and he asked her about her new girl. To his surprise the good lady was unusually reticent. She couldn't really say very much about Nelly. No, she didn't belong anywhere near Riverside. In fact, she – Mrs. Pennington – didn't think she had any settled home at present. Her father was travelling over the country somewhere. Nelly was a good little girl, and very obliging. Beyond this Winslow could get no more information, so he went around and talked to Nelly, who was sitting on the bench under the poplars and seemed absorbed in watching the sunset.

She dropped her g's badly and made some grammatical errors that caused Winslow's flesh to creep on his bones. But any man could have forgiven mistakes from such dimpled lips in such a sweet voice.

He asked her to go for a row up the river in the twilight and she assented; she handled an oar very well, he found out, and the exercise became her. Winslow tried to get her to talk about herself, but failed signally and had to content himself with Mrs. Pennington's meagre information. He told her about himself frankly enough – how he had had fever in the spring and had been ordered to spend the summer in the country and do nothing useful until his health was fully restored, and how lonesome it was in Riverside in general and at the Beckwith farm in particular. He made out quite a dismal case for himself and if Nelly wasn't sorry for him, she should have been.

AT THE END OF A FORTNIGHT Riverside folks began to talk about Winslow and the Penningtons' hired girl. He was reported to be "dead gone" on her; he took her out rowing every evening, drove her to preaching up the Bend on Sunday nights, and haunted the Pennington farmhouse. Wise folks shook their heads over it and wondered that Mrs. Pennington allowed it. Winslow was a gentleman, and that Nelly Ray, whom nobody knew anything about, not even where she came from, was only a common hired girl, and he had no business to be hanging about her. She was pretty, to be sure; but she was absurdly stuck-up and wouldn't associate with other Riverside "help" at all. Well, pride must have a fall; there must be something queer about her when she was so awful sly as to her past life.

Winslow and Nelly did not trouble themselves in the least over all this gossip; in fact, they never even heard it. Winslow was hopelessly in love; when he found this out he was aghast. He thought of his father, the ambitious railroad magnate; of his mother, the brilliant society leader; of his sisters, the beautiful and proud; he was honestly frightened. It would never do; he must not go to see Nelly again. He kept this prudent resolution for twenty-four hours and then rowed over to the West shore. He found Nelly sitting on the bank in her old faded print dress and he straightway forgot everything he ought to have remembered.

Nelly herself never seemed to be conscious of the social gulf between them. At least she never alluded to it in any way, and accepted Winslow's attentions as if she had a perfect right to them. She had broken the record by staying with Mrs.

Pennington four weeks, and even the cats were in subjection.

Winslow was well enough to have gone back to the city and, in fact, his father was writing for him. But he couldn't leave Beckwiths', apparently. At any rate he stayed on and met Nelly every day and cursed himself for a cad and a cur and a weak-brained idiot.

One day he took Nelly for a row up the river. They went further than usual around the Bend. Winslow didn't want to go too far, for he knew that a party of his city friends, chaperoned by Mrs. Keyton-Wells, were having a picnic somewhere up along the river shore that day. But Nelly insisted on going on and on, and of course she had her way. When they reached a little pine-fringed headland they came upon the picnickers, within a stone's throw. Everybody recognized Winslow. "Why, there is Burton!" he heard Mrs. Keyton-Wells exclaim, and he knew she was putting up her glasses. Will Evans, who was an especial chum of his, ran down to the water's edge. "Bless me, Win, where did you come from? Come right in. We haven't had tea yet. Bring your friend too," he added, becoming conscious that Winslow's friend was a mighty pretty girl. Winslow's face was crimson. He avoided Nelly's eye.

"Are them people friends of yours?" she asked in a low tone.

"Yes," he muttered.

"Well, let us go ashore if they want us to," she said calmly. "I don't mind."

For three seconds Winslow hesitated. Then he pulled ashore and helped Nelly to alight on a jutting rock. There was a curious, set expression about his fine mouth as he marched Nelly up to Mrs. Keyton-Wells and introduced her. Mrs. Keyton-Wells's greeting was slightly cool, but very polite. She supposed Miss Ray was some little country girl with whom Burton Winslow was carrying on a summer flirtation; respectable enough, no doubt, and must be treated civilly, but of course wouldn't expect to be made an equal of exactly. The other women took their cue from her, but the men were more cordial. Miss Ray might be shabby, but she was distinctly fetching, and Winslow looked savage.

Nelly was not a whit abashed, seemingly, by the fashionable circle in which she found herself, and she talked away to Will Evans and the others in her soft drawl as if she had known them all her life. All might have gone passably well, had not a little Riverside imp, by name of Rufus Hent, who had been picked up by the picnickers to run their errands, come up just then with a pail of water.

"Golly!" he ejaculated in very audible tones. "If there ain't Mrs. Pennington's hired girl!"

Mrs. Keyton-Wells stiffened with horror. Winslow darted a furious glance at the tell-tale that would have annihilated anything except a small boy. Will Evans grinned and went on talking to Nelly, who had failed to hear, or at least to heed, the exclamation.

The mischief was done; the social thermometer went down to zero in Nelly's neighbourhood. The women ignored her altogether. Winslow set his teeth together and registered a mental vow to wring Rufus Hent's sunburned neck at the first opportunity. He escorted Nelly to the table and waited on her with ostentatious deference, while Mrs. Keyton-Wells glanced at him stonily and made up her mind to tell his mother when she went home.

Nelly's social ostracism did not affect her appetite. But after lunch was over, she walked down to the skiff. Winslow followed her.

"Do you want to go home?" he asked.

"Yes, it's time I went, for the cats may be raidin' the pantry. But you must not come; your friends here want you."

"Nonsense!" said Winslow sulkily. "If you are going I am too."

But Nelly was too quick for him; she sprang into the skiff, unwound the rope, and pushed off before he guessed her intention.

"I can row myself home and I mean to," she announced, taking up the oars defiantly.

"Nelly," he implored.

Nelly looked at him wickedly.

"You'd better go back to your friends. That old woman with the eyeglasses is watchin' you."

Winslow said something strong under his breath as he went back to the others. Will Evans and his chums began to chaff him about Nelly, but he looked so dangerous that they concluded to stop. There is no denying that Winslow was in a fearful temper just then with Mrs. Keyton-Wells, Evans, himself, Nelly – in fact, with all the world.

His friends drove him home in the evening on their way to the station and dropped him at the Beckwith farm. At dusk he went moodily down to the shore. Far up the Bend was dim and shadowy and stars were shining above the wooded shores. Over the river the Pennington farmhouse lights twinkled out alluringly. Winslow watched them until he could stand it no longer. Nelly had made off with his skiff, but Perry Beckwith's dory was ready to hand. In five minutes, Winslow was grounding her on the West shore. Nelly was sitting on a rock at the landing place. He went over and sat down silently beside her. A full moon was rising above the dark hills up the Bend and in the faint light the girl was wonderfully lovely.

"I thought you weren't comin' over at all tonight," she said, smiling up at him, "and I was sorry, because I wanted to say goodbye to you."

"Goodbye? Nelly, you're not going away?"

"Yes. The cats were in the pantry when I got home."

"Nelly!"

"Well, to be serious. I'm not goin' for that, but I really am goin'. I had a letter from Dad this evenin'. Did you have a good time after I left this afternoon? Did Mrs. Keyton-Wells thaw out?"

"Hang Mrs. Keyton-Wells! Nelly, where are you going?"

"To Dad, of course. We used to live down south together, but two months ago we broke up housekeepin' and come north. We thought we could do better up here, you know. Dad started out to look for a place to settle down and I came here while he was prospectin'. He's got a house now, he says, and wants me to go right off. I'm goin' tomorrow."

"Nelly, you mustn't go – you mustn't, I tell you," exclaimed Winslow in despair. "I love you – I love you – you must stay with me forever."

"You don't know what you're sayin', Mr. Winslow," said Nelly coldly. "Why, you can't marry me – a common servant girl."

"I can and I will, if you'll have me," answered Winslow recklessly. "I can't ever let you go. I've loved you ever since I first saw you. Nelly, won't you be my wife? Don't you love me?"

"Well, yes, I do," confessed Nelly suddenly; and then it was fully five minutes before Winslow gave her a chance to say anything else.

"Oh, what will your people say?" she contrived to ask at last. "Won't they be in a dreadful state? Oh, it will never do for you to marry me."

"Won't it?" said Winslow in a tone of satisfaction. "I rather think it will. Of course, my family will rampage a bit at first. I daresay Father'll turn me out. Don't worry over that, Nelly. I'm not afraid of work. I'm not afraid of anything except losing you."

"You'll have to see what Dad says," remarked Nelly, after another eloquent interlude.

"He won't object, will he? I'll write to him or go and see him. Where is he?"

"He is in town at the Arlington."

"The Arlington!" Winslow was amazed. The Arlington was the most exclusive and expensive hotel in town.

"What is he doing there?"

"Transacting a real estate or railroad deal with your father, I believe, or something of that sort."

"Nelly!"

"Well?"

"What do you mean?"

"Just what I say."

Winslow got up and looked at her.

"Nelly, who are you?"

"Helen Ray Scott, at your service, sir."

"Not Helen Ray Scott, the daughter of the railroad king?"

"The same. Are you sorry that you're engaged to her? If you are, she'll stay Nelly Ray."

Winslow dropped back on the seat with a long breath.

"Nelly, I don't understand. Why did you deceive me? I feel stunned."

"Oh, do forgive me," she said merrily. "I shouldn't have, I suppose – but you know you took me for the hired girl the very first time you saw me, and you patronized me and called me Nelly; so I let you think so just for fun. I never thought it would come to this. When Father and I came north I took a fancy to come here and stay with Mrs. Pennington – who is an old nurse of mine – until Father decided where to take up our abode. I got here the night before we met. My trunk was delayed so I put on an old cotton dress her niece had left here – and you came and saw me. I made Mrs. Pennington keep the secret – she thought it great fun; and I really was a great hand to do little chores and keep the cats in subjection too. I made mistakes in grammar and dropped my g's on purpose – it was such fun to see you wince when I did it. It was cruel to tease you so, I suppose, but it was so sweet just to be loved for myself – not because I was an heiress and a belle – I couldn't bear to tell you the truth. Did you think I couldn't read your thoughts this afternoon, when I insisted on going ashore? You were a little ashamed of me – you know you were. I didn't blame you for that, but if you hadn't gone ashore and taken me as you did I would never have spoken to you again. Mrs. Keyton-Wells won't snub me next time we meet. And some way I don't think your father will turn you out, either. Have you forgiven me yet, Burton?"

"I shall never call you anything but Nelly," said Winslow irrelevantly.

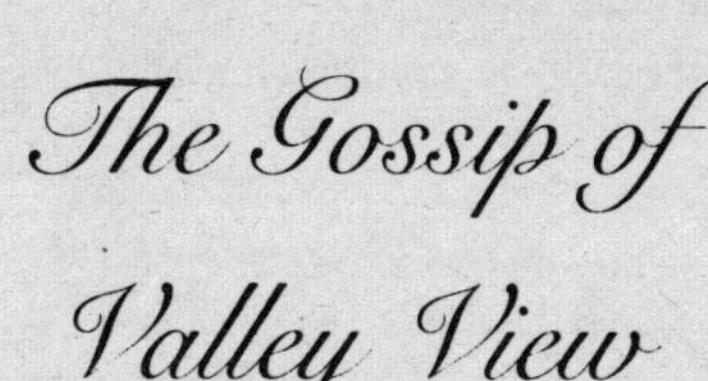
The Gossip of
Valley View

T WAS the first of April, and Julius Barrett, aged fourteen, perched on his father's gatepost, watched ruefully the low descending sun, and counted that day lost. He had not succeeded in "fooling" a single person, although he had tried repeatedly. One and all, old and young, of his intended victims had been too wary for Julius. Hence, Julius was disgusted and ready for anything in the way of a stratagem or a spoil.

The Barrett gatepost topped the highest hill in Valley View. Julius could see the entire settlement, from "Young" Thomas Everett's farm, a mile to the west, to Adelia Williams's weather-grey little house on a moonrise slope to the east. He was gazing moodily down the muddy road when Dan Chester, homeward bound from the post office, came riding sloppily along on his grey mare and pulled up by the Barrett gate to hand a paper to Julius.

Dan was a young man who took life and himself very seriously. He seldom smiled, never joked, and had a Washingtonian reputation for veracity. Dan had never told a conscious falsehood in his life; he never even exaggerated.

Julius, beholding Dan's solemn face, was seized with a perfectly irresistible desire to "fool" him. At the same moment his eye caught the dazzling reflection of the setting sun on the windows of Adelia Williams's house, and he had an inspiration little short of diabolical. "Have you heard the news, Dan?" he asked.

"No, what is it?" asked Dan.

"I dunno's I ought to tell it," said Julius reflectively. "It's kind of a family affair, but then Adelia didn't say not to, and anyway it'll be all over the place soon. So I'll tell you, Dan, if you'll promise never to tell who told you. Adelia Williams and Young Thomas Everett are going to be married."

Julius delivered himself of this tremendous lie with a

transparently earnest countenance. Yet Dan, credulous as he was, could not believe it all at once.

"Git out," he said.

"It's true, 'pon my word," protested Julius. "Adelia was up last night and told Ma all about it. Ma's her cousin, you know. The wedding is to be in June, and Adelia asked Ma to help her get her quilts and things ready."

Julius reeled all this off so glibly that Dan finally believed the story, despite the fact that the people thus coupled together in prospective matrimony were the very last people in Valley View who could have been expected to marry each other. Young Thomas was a confirmed bachelor of fifty, and Adelia Williams was forty; they were not supposed to be even well acquainted, as the Everetts and the Williamses had never been very friendly, although no open feud existed between them.

Nevertheless, in view of Julius's circumstantial statements, the amazing news must be true, and Dan was instantly agog to carry it further. Julius watched Dan and the grey mare out of sight, fairly writhing with ecstasy. Oh, but Dan had been easy! The story would be all over Valley View in twenty-four hours. Julius laughed until he came near to falling off the gatepost.

At this point Julius and Danny drop out of our story, and Young Thomas enters.

It was two days later when Young Thomas heard that he was to be married to Adelia Williams in June. Eben Clark, the blacksmith, told him when he went to the forge to get his horse shod. Young Thomas laughed his big jolly laugh. Valley View gossip had been marrying him off for the last thirty years, although never before to Adelia Williams.

"It's news to me," he said tolerantly.

Eben grinned broadly. "Ah, you can't bluff it off like that, Tom," he said. "The news came too straight this time. Well, I was glad to hear it, although I was mighty surprised. I never thought of you and Adelia. But she's a fine little woman and will make you a capital wife."

Young Thomas grunted and drove away. He had a good deal of business to do that day, involving calls at various places – the store for molasses, the mill for flour, Jim Bentley's for seed grain, the doctor's for toothache drops for his housekeeper, the post office for mail – and at each and every place he was joked about his approaching marriage. In the end it rather annoyed Young Thomas. He drove home at last in what was for him something of a temper. How on earth had that fool story started? With such detailed circumstantiality of rugs and quilts, too? Adelia Williams must be going to marry somebody, and the Valley View gossips, unable to locate the man, had guessed Young Thomas.

When he reached home, tired, mud-bespattered, and hungry, his housekeeper, who was also his hired man's wife, asked him if it was true that he was going to be married. Young Thomas, taking in at a glance the ill-prepared, half-cold supper on the table, felt more annoyed than ever, and said it wasn't, with a strong expression – not quite an oath – for Young Thomas never swore, unless swearing be as much a matter of intonation as of words.

Mrs. Dunn sighed, patted her swelled face, and said she was sorry; she had hoped it was true, for her man had decided to go west. They were to go in a month's time. Young Thomas sat down to his supper with the prospect of having to look up another housekeeper and hired man before planting to destroy his appetite.

Next day, three people who came to see Young Thomas on business congratulated him on his approaching marriage. Young Thomas, who had recovered his usual good humour, merely laughed. There was no use in being too earnest in denial, he thought. He knew that his unusual fit of petulance with his housekeeper had only convinced her that the story was true. It would die away in time, as other similar stories had died, he thought. Valley View gossip was imaginative.

Young Thomas looked rather serious, however, when the minister and his wife called that evening and referred to the report. Young Thomas gravely said that it was unfounded. The minister looked graver still and said he was sorry – he had hoped it was true. His wife glanced significantly about Young Thomas's big, untidy sitting-room, where there were cobwebs on the ceiling and fluff in the corners and dust on the mop-board, and said nothing, but looked volumes.

"Dang it all," said Young Thomas, as they drove away, "they'll marry me yet in spite of myself."

The gossip made him think about Adelia Williams. He had never thought about her before; he was barely acquainted with her. Now he remembered that she was a plump, jolly-looking little woman, noted for being a good housekeeper. Then Young Thomas groaned, remembering that he must start out looking for a housekeeper soon; and housekeepers were not easily found, as Young Thomas had discovered several times since his mother's death ten years before.

Next Sunday in church Young Thomas looked at Adelia Williams. He caught Adelia looking at him. Adelia blushed and looked guiltily away.

"Dang it all," reflected Young Thomas, forgetting that he was in church. "I suppose she has heard that fool story too. I'd like to know the person who started it; man or woman, I'd punch their head."

Nevertheless, Young Thomas went on looking at Adelia by fits and starts, although he did not again catch Adelia looking at him. He noticed that she had round rosy cheeks and twinkling brown eyes. She did not look like an old maid, and Young Thomas wondered that she had been allowed to become one. Sarah Barnett, now, to whom report had married him a year ago, looked like a dried sour apple.

FOR THE NEXT FOUR WEEKS the story haunted Young Thomas like a spectre. Down it would not. Everywhere he went he was joked about it. It gathered fresh detail every week. Adelia was getting her clothes ready; she was to be married in seal-brown cashmere; Vinnie Lawrence at Valley Centre was making it for her; she had got a new hat with a long ostrich plume; some said white, some said grey.

Young Thomas kept wondering who the man could be, for he was convinced that Adelia was going to marry somebody. More than that, once he caught himself wondering enviously. Adelia was a nice-looking woman, and he had not so far heard of any probable housekeeper.

"Dang it all," said Young Thomas to himself in desperation. "I wouldn't care if it was true."

His married sister from Carlisle heard the story and came over to investigate. Young Thomas denied it shortly, and his sister scolded. She had devoutly hoped it was true, she said, and it would have been a great weight off her mind.

"This house is in a disgraceful condition, Thomas," she said severely. "It would break Mother's heart if she could rise out of her grave to see it. And Adelia Williams is a perfect housekeeper."

"You didn't use to think so much of the Williams crowd," said Young Thomas drily.

"Oh, some of them don't amount to much," admitted Maria, "but Adelia is all right."

Catching sight of an odd look on Young Thomas's face, she added hastily, "Thomas Everett, I believe it's true after all. Now, is it? For mercy's sake don't be so sly. You might tell me, your own and only sister, if it is."

"Oh, shut up," was Young Thomas's unfeeling reply to his own and only sister.

Young Thomas told himself that night that Valley View gossip would drive him into an asylum yet if it didn't let up. He also wondered if Adelia was as much persecuted as himself. No doubt she was. He never could catch her eye in church now, but he would have been surprised had he realized how many times he tried to.

The climax came the third week in May, when Young Thomas, who had been keeping house for himself for three weeks, received a letter and an express box from his cousin, Charles Everett, out in Manitoba. Charles and he had been chums in their boyhood. They corresponded occasionally still, although it was twenty years since Charles had gone west.

The letter was to congratulate Young Thomas on his approaching marriage. Charles had heard of it through some Valley View correspondents of his wife. He was much pleased; he had always liked Adelia, he said – had been an old beau of hers, in fact. Thomas might give her a kiss for him if he liked. He forwarded a wedding present by express and hoped they would be very happy, etc.

The present was an elaborate hatrack of polished buffalo horns, mounted on red plush, with an inset mirror. Young Thomas set it up on the kitchen table and scowled moodily at his reflection in the mirror. If wedding presents were beginning to come, it was high time something was done. The matter was past being a joke. This affair of the present would certainly get out – things always got out in Valley View, dang it all – and he would never hear the last of it.

"I'll marry," said Young Thomas decisively. "If Adelia Williams won't have me, I'll marry the first woman who will, if it's Sarah Barnett herself."

Young Thomas shaved and put on his Sunday suit. As soon as it was safely dark, he hied him away to Adelia Williams. He felt very doubtful about his reception, but the remembrance of the twinkle in Adelia's brown eyes comforted him. She looked like a woman who had a sense of humour; she might not take him, but she would not feel offended or insulted because he asked her.

"Dang it all, though, I hope she will take me," said Young Thomas. "I'm in for getting married now and no mistake. And I can't get Adelia out of my head. I've been thinking of her steady ever since that confounded gossip began."

When he knocked at Adelia's door he discovered that his face was wet with perspiration. Adelia opened the door and started when she saw him; then she turned very red and stiffly asked him in. Young Thomas went in and sat down, wondering if all men felt so horribly uncomfortable when they went courting.

Adelia stooped low over the woodbox to put a stick of wood in the stove, for the May evening was chilly. Her shoulders were shaking; the shaking grew worse; suddenly Adelia laughed hysterically and, sitting down on the woodbox, continued to laugh. Young Thomas eyed her with a friendly grin.

"Oh, do excuse me," gasped poor Adelia, wiping tears from her eyes. "This is – dreadful – I didn't mean to laugh – I don't know why I'm laughing – but – I – can't help it."

She laughed helplessly again. Young Thomas laughed too. His embarrassment vanished in the mellowness of that laughter. Presently Adelia composed herself and removed from the woodbox to a chair, but there was still a suspicious twitching about the corners of her mouth.

"I suppose," said Young Thomas, determined to have it over with before the ice could form again, "I suppose, Adelia, you've heard the story that's been going about you and me of late?"

Adelia nodded. "I've been persecuted to the verge of insanity with it," she said. "Every soul I've seen has tormented me about it, and people have written me about it. I've denied it till I was black in the face, but nobody believed me. I can't find out how it started. I hope you believe, Mr. Everett, that it couldn't possibly have arisen from anything I said. I've felt dreadfully worried for fear you might think it did. I heard that my cousin, Lucilla Barrett, said I told her, but Lucilla vowed to me that she never said such a thing or even dreamed of it. I've felt dreadful bad over the whole affair. I even gave up the idea of making a quilt after a lovely new pattern I've got, because they made such a talk about my brown dress."

"I've been kind of supposing that you must be going to marry somebody, and folks just guessed it was me," said Young Thomas – he said it anxiously.

"No, I'm not going to be married to anybody," said Adelia with a laugh, taking up her knitting.

"I'm glad of that," said Young Thomas gravely. "I mean," he hastened to add, seeing the look of astonishment on Adelia's face, "that I'm glad there isn't any other man – because – because I want you myself, Adelia."

Adelia laid down her knitting and blushed crimson. But she looked at Young Thomas squarely and reproachfully.

"You needn't think you are bound to say that because of the gossip, Mr. Everett," she said quietly.

"Oh, I don't," said Young Thomas earnestly. "But the truth is, the story set me to thinking about you, and from that I got to wishing it was true – honest, I did – I couldn't get you out of my head, and at last I didn't want to. It just seemed to me that you were the very woman for me if you'd only take me. Will you, Adelia? I've got a good farm and house, and I'll try to make you happy."

It was not a very romantic wooing, perhaps. But Adelia was forty and had never been a romantic little body even in the heyday of youth. She was a practical woman, and Young Thomas was a fine looking man of his age with abundance of worldly goods. Besides, she liked him, and the gossip had made her think a good deal about him of late. Indeed, in a moment of candour she had owned to herself the very last Sunday in church that she wouldn't mind if the story were true.

"I'll – I'll think of it," she said.

This was practically an acceptance, and Young Thomas so

understood it. Without loss of time he crossed the kitchen, sat down beside Adelia, and put his arms about her plump waist.

"Here's a kiss Charlie sent me to give you," he said, giving it.

The Pursuit of the Ideal

REDA'S snuggery was aglow with the rose-red splendour of an open fire which was triumphantly warding off the stealthy approaches of the dull grey autumn twilight. Roger St. Clair stretched himself out luxuriously in an easy-chair with a sigh of pleasure.

"Freda, your armchairs are the most comfy in the world. How do you get them to fit into a fellow's kinks so splendidly?"

Freda smiled at him out of big, owlish eyes that were the same tint as the coppery grey sea upon which the north window of the snuggery looked.

"Any armchair will fit a lazy fellow's kinks," she said.

"I'm not lazy," protested Roger. "That you should say so, Freda, when I have wheeled all the way out of town this dismal afternoon over the worst bicycle road in three kingdoms to see you, bonnie maid!"

"I like lazy people," said Freda softly, tilting her spoon on a cup of chocolate with a slender brown hand.

Roger smiled at her chummily.

"You are such a comfortable girl," he said. "I like to talk to you and tell you things."

"You have something to tell me today. It has been fairly sticking out of your eyes ever since you came. Now, 'fess."

Freda put away her cup and saucer, got up, and stood by the fireplace, with one arm outstretched along the quaintly carved old mantel. She laid her head down on its curve and looked expectantly at Roger.

"I have seen my ideal, Freda," said Roger gravely.

Freda lifted her head and then laid it down again. She did not speak. Roger was glad of it. Even at the moment he found himself thinking that Freda had a genius for silence. Any other girl he knew would have broken in at once with surprised exclamations and questions and spoiled his story.

"You have not forgotten what my ideal woman is like?" he said.

Freda shook her head. She was not likely to forget. She remembered only too keenly the afternoon he had told her. They had been sitting in the snuggery, herself in the ingle-nook, and Roger coiled up in his big pet chair that nobody else ever sat in.

"'What must my lady be that I must love her?'" he had quoted. "Well, I will paint my dream-love for you, Freda. She must be tall and slender, with chestnut hair of wonderful gloss, with just the suggestion of a ripple in it. She must have an oval face, colourless ivory in hue, with the expression of a Madonna; and her eyes must be 'passionless, peaceful blue,' deep and tender as a twilight sky."

Freda, looking at herself along her arm in the mirror, recalled this description and smiled faintly. She was short and plump, with a piquant, irregular little face, vivid tinting, curly, unmanageable hair of ruddy brown, and big grey eyes. Certainly, she was not his ideal.

"When and where did you meet your lady of the Madonna face and twilight eyes?" she asked.

Roger frowned. Freda's face was solemn enough but her eyes looked as if she might be laughing at him.

"I haven't met her yet. I have only seen her. It was in the park yesterday. She was in a carriage with the Mandersons. So beautiful, Freda! Our eyes met as she drove past and I realized that I had found my long-sought ideal. I rushed back to town and hunted up Pete Manderson at the club. Pete is a donkey but he has his ways of being useful. He told me who she was. Her name is Stephanie Gardiner; she is his cousin from the south and is visiting his mother. And, Freda, I am to dine at the Mandersons' tonight. I shall meet her."

"Do goddesses and ideals and Madonnas eat?" said Freda in an awed whisper. Her eyes were certainly laughing now. Roger got up stiffly.

"I must confess I did not expect that you would ridicule my confidence, Freda," he said frigidly. "It is very unlike you. But if you are not interested I will not bore you with any further details. And it is time I was getting back to town anyhow."

When he had gone Freda ran to the west window and flung it open. She leaned out and waved both hands at him over the spruce hedge.

"Roger, Roger, I was a horrid little beast. Forget it immediately, please. And come out tomorrow and tell me all about her."

Roger came. He bored Freda terribly with his raptures but she never betrayed it. She was all sympathy – or, at least, as much sympathy as a woman can be who must listen while the man of men sings another woman's praises to her. She sent Roger away in perfect good humour with himself and all the world, then she curled herself up in the snuggery, pulled a rug over her head, and cried.

Roger came out to Lowlands oftener than ever after that. He had to talk to somebody about Stephanie Gardiner and Freda was the safest vent. The "pursuit of the Ideal," as she called it, went on with vim and fervour. Sometimes Roger would be on the heights of hope and elation; the next visit he would be in the depths of despair and humility. Freda had learned to tell which it was by the way he opened the snuggery door.

One day when Roger came he found six feet of young man reposing at ease in his particular chair. Freda was sipping chocolate in her corner and looking over the rim of her cup at the intruder just as she had been wont to look at Roger. She had on a new dark red gown and looked vivid and rose-hued.

She introduced the stranger as Mr. Grayson and called him Tim. They seemed to be excellent friends. Roger sat bolt upright on the edge of a fragile, gilded chair which Freda kept to hide a shabby spot in the carpet, and glared at Tim until the latter said goodbye and lounged out.

"You'll be over tomorrow?" said Freda.

"Can't I come this evening?" he pleaded.

Freda nodded. "Yes – and we'll make taffy. You used to make such delicious stuff, Tim."

"Who is that fellow, Freda?" Roger inquired crossly, as soon as the door closed.

Freda began to make a fresh pot of chocolate. She smiled dreamily as if thinking of something pleasant.

"Why, that was Tim Grayson – dear old Tim. He used to live next door to us when we were children. And we were such chums – always together, making mud pies, and getting into scrapes. He is just the same old Tim, and is home from the west for a long visit. I was so glad to see him again."

"So it would appear," said Roger grumpily. "Well, now that 'dear old Tim' is gone, I suppose I can have my own chair, can I? And do give me some chocolate. I didn't know you made taffy."

"Oh, I don't. It's Tim. He can do everything. He used to make it long ago, and I washed up after him and helped him eat it. How is the pursuit of the Ideal coming on, Roger-boy?"

Roger did not feel as if he wanted to talk about the Ideal. He noticed how vivid Freda's smile was and how lovable were the curves of her neck where the dusky curls were caught up from it. He had also an inner vision of Freda making taffy with Tim and he did not approve of it.

He refused to talk about the Ideal. On his way back to town he found himself thinking that Freda had the most charming, glad little laugh of any girl he knew. He suddenly remembered that he had never heard the Ideal laugh. She smiled placidly – he had raved to Freda about that smile – but she did not laugh. Roger began to wonder what an ideal without any sense of humour would be like when translated into the real.

He went to Lowlands the next afternoon and found Tim there – in his chair again. He detested the fellow but he could not deny that he was good-looking and had charming manners. Freda was very nice to Tim. On his way back to town Roger decided that Tim was in love with Freda. He was furious at the idea. The presumption of the man!

He also remembered that he had not said a word to Freda about the Ideal. And he never did say much more – perhaps because he could not get the chance. Tim was always there before him and generally outstayed him.

One day when he went out he did not find Freda at home. Her aunt told him that she was out riding with Mr. Grayson. On his way back he met them. As they cantered by, Freda waved her riding whip at him. Her face was full of warm, ripe, kissable tints, her loose lovelocks were blowing about it, and her eyes shone like grey pools mirroring stars. Roger turned and watched them out of sight behind the firs that cupped Lowlands.

That night at Mrs. Crandall's dinner table somebody began to talk about Freda. Roger strained his ears to listen. Mrs. Kitty Carr was speaking – Mrs. Kitty knew everything and everybody.

"She is simply the most charming girl in the world when you get really acquainted with her," said Mrs. Kitty, with the air of having discovered and patented Freda. "She is so vivid and unconventional and lovable – 'spirit and fire and dew,' you know. Tim Grayson is a very lucky fellow."

"Are they engaged?" someone asked.

"Not yet, I fancy. But of course it is only a question of time. Tim simply adores her. He is a good soul and has lots of money, so he'll do. But really, you know, I think a prince wouldn't be good enough for Freda."

Roger suddenly became conscious that the Ideal was asking him a question of which he had not heard a word. He apologized and was forgiven. But he went home a very miserable man.

He did not go to Lowlands for two weeks. They were the longest, most wretched two weeks he had ever lived through. One afternoon he heard that Tim Grayson had gone back west. Mrs. Kitty told it mournfully.

"Of course, this means that Freda has refused him," she said. "She is such an odd girl."

Roger went straight out to Lowlands. He found Freda in the snuggery and held out his hands to her.

"Freda, will you marry me? It will take a lifetime to tell you how much I love you."

"But the Ideal?" questioned Freda.

"I have just discovered what my ideal is," said Roger. "She is a dear, loyal, companionable little girl, with the jolliest laugh and the warmest, truest heart in the world. She has starry grey eyes, two dimples, and a mouth I must and will kiss – there – there – there! Freda, tell me you love me a little bit, although I've been such a besotted idiot."

"I will not let you call my husband-that-is-to-be names," said Freda, snuggling down into the curve of his shoulder. "But indeed, Roger-boy, you will have to make me very, very happy to square matters up. You have made me so unutterably unhappy for two months."

"The pursuit of the Ideal is ended," declared Roger.

By the Rule of Contrary

ook here, Burton," said old John Ellis in an ominous tone of voice, "I want to know if what that old busybody of a Mary Keane came here today gossiping about is true. If it is – well, I've something to say about the matter! Have you been courting that niece of Susan Oliver's all summer on the sly?"

Burton Ellis's handsome, boyish face flushed darkly crimson to the roots of his curly black hair. Something in the father's tone roused anger and rebellion in the son. He straightened himself up from the turnip row he was hoeing, looked his father squarely in the face, and said quietly,

"Not on the sly, sir. I never do things that way. But I have been going to see Madge Oliver for some time, and we are engaged. We are thinking of being married this fall, and we hope you will not object."

Burton's frankness nearly took away his father's breath. Old John fairly choked with rage.

"You young fool," he spluttered, bringing down his hoe with such energy that he sliced off half a dozen of his finest young turnip plants, "have you gone clean crazy? No, sir, I'll never consent to your marrying an Oliver, and you needn't have any idea that I will."

"Then I'll marry her without your consent," retorted Burton angrily, losing the temper he had been trying to keep.

"Oh, will you indeed! Well, if you do, out you go, and not a cent of my money or a rod of my land do you ever get."

"What have you got against Madge?" asked Burton, forcing himself to speak calmly, for he knew his father too well to doubt for a minute that he meant and would do just what he said.

"She's an Oliver," said old John crustily, "and that's enough." And considering that he had settled the matter, John Ellis threw down his hoe and left the field in a towering rage.

Burton hoed away savagely until his anger had spent itself on the weeds. Give up Madge – dear, sweet little Madge? Not he! Yet if his father remained of the same mind, their marriage was out of the question at present. And Burton knew quite well that his father would remain of the same mind. Old John Ellis had the reputation of being the most contrary man in Greenwood.

When Burton had finished his row he left the turnip field and went straight across lots to see Madge and tell her his dismal story. An hour later Miss Susan Oliver went up the stairs of her little brown house to Madge's room and found her niece lying on the bed, her pretty curls tumbled, her soft cheeks flushed crimson, crying as if her heart would break.

Miss Susan was a tall, grim, angular spinster who looked like the last person in the world to whom a love affair might be confided. But never were appearances more deceptive than in this case. Behind her unprepossessing exterior Miss Susan had a warm, sympathetic heart filled to the brim with kindly affection for her pretty niece. She had seen Burton Ellis going moodily across the fields homeward and guessed that something had gone wrong.

"Now, dearie, what is the matter?" she said, tenderly patting the brown head.

Madge sobbed out the whole story disconsolately. Burton's father would not let him marry her because she was an Oliver. And, oh, what would she do?

"Don't worry, Madge," said Miss Susan comfortingly. "I'll soon settle old John Ellis."

"Why, what can you do?" asked Madge forlornly.

Miss Susan squared her shoulders and looked amused.

"You'll see. I know old John Ellis better than he knows himself. He is the most contrary man the Lord ever made. I went to school with him. I learned how to manage him then, and I haven't forgotten how. I'm going straight up to interview him."

"Are you sure that will do any good?" said Madge doubtfully. "If you go to him and take Burton's and my part, won't it only make him worse?"

"Madge, dear," said Miss Susan, busily twisting her scanty, iron-grey hair up into a hard little knob at the back of her head before Madge's glass, "you just wait. I'm not young, and I'm not pretty, and I'm not in love, but I've more gumption than you and Burton have or ever will have. You keep your eyes open and see if you can learn something. You'll need it if you go up to live with old John Ellis."

Burton had returned to the turnip field, but old John Ellis was taking his ease with a rampant political newspaper on the cool verandah of his house. Looking up from a bitter editorial to chuckle over a cutting sarcasm contained therein, he saw a tall, angular figure coming up the lane with aggressiveness written large in every fold and flutter of shawl and skirt.

"Old Susan Oliver, as sure as a gun," said old John with another chuckle. "She looks mad clean through. I suppose she's coming here to blow me up for refusing to let Burton take that girl of hers. She's been angling and scheming for it for years, but she will find who she has to deal with. Come on, Miss Susan."

John Ellis laid down his paper and stood up with a sarcastic smile.

Miss Susan reached the steps and skimmed undauntedly up them. She did indeed look angry and disturbed. Without any preliminary greeting she burst out into a tirade that simply took away her complacent foe's breath.

"Look here, John Ellis, I want to know what this means. I've discovered that that young upstart of a son of yours, who ought to be in short trousers yet, has been courting my niece, Madge Oliver, all summer. He has had the impudence to tell me that he wants to marry her. I won't have it, I tell you, and you can tell your son so. Marry my niece indeed! A pretty pass the world is coming to! I'll never consent to it."

Perhaps if you had searched Greenwood and all the adjacent districts thoroughly you might have found a man who was more astonished and taken aback than old John Ellis was at that moment, but I doubt it. The wind was completely taken out of his sails and every bit of the Ellis contrariness was roused.

"What have you got to say against my son?" he fairly shouted in his rage. "Isn't he good enough for your girl, Susan Oliver, I'd like to know?"

"No, he isn't," retorted Miss Susan deliberately and unflinchingly. "He's well enough in his place, but you'll please to remember, John Ellis, that my niece is an Oliver, and the Olivers don't marry beneath them."

Old John was furious. "Beneath them indeed! Why, woman, it is condescension in my son to so much as look at your niece – condescension, that is what it is. You are as poor as church mice."

"We come of good family, though," retorted Miss Susan. "You Ellises are nobodies. Your grandfather was a hired man! And yet you have the presumption to think you're fit to marry into an old, respectable family like the Olivers. But talking doesn't signify. I simply won't allow this nonsense to go on. I came here today to tell you so plump and plain. It's your duty to stop it; if you don't I will, that's all."

"Oh, will you?" John Ellis was at a white heat of rage and stubbornness now. "We'll see, Miss Susan, we'll see. My son shall marry whatever girl he pleases, and I'll back him up in it – do you hear that? Come here and tell me my son isn't good enough for your niece indeed! I'll show you he can get her, anyway."

"You've heard what I've said," was the answer, "and you'd better go by it, that's all. I shan't stay to bandy words with you, John Ellis. I'm going home to talk to my niece and tell her her duty plain, and what I want her to do, and she'll do it, I haven't a fear."

Miss Susan was halfway down the steps, but John Ellis ran to the railing of the verandah to get the last word.

"I'll send Burton down this evening to talk to her and tell her what *he* wants her to do, and we'll see whether she'll sooner listen to you than to him," he shouted.

Miss Susan deigned no reply. Old John strode out to the turnip field. Burton saw him coming and looked for another outburst of wrath, but his father's first words almost took away his breath.

"See here, Burt, I take back all I said this afternoon. I want you to marry Madge Oliver now, and the sooner, the better. That old cat of a Susan had the face to come up and tell me you weren't good enough for her niece. I told her a few plain truths. Don't you mind the old crosspatch. I'll back you up."

By this time Burton had begun hoeing vigorously, to hide the amused twinkle of comprehension in his eyes. He admired Miss Susan's tactics, but he did not say so.

"All right, Father," he answered dutifully.

When Miss Susan reached home she told Madge to bathe her eyes and put on her new pink muslin, because she guessed Burton would be down that evening.

"Oh, Auntie, how did you manage it?" cried Madge.

"Madge," said Miss Susan solemnly, but with dancing eyes, "do you know how to drive a pig? Just try to make it go in the opposite direction and it will bolt the way you want it. Remember that, my dear."

Nan

AN was polishing the tumblers at the pantry window, outside of which John Osborne was leaning among the vines. His arms were folded on the sill and his straw hat was pushed back from his flushed, eager face as he watched Nan's deft movements.

Beyond them, old Abe Stewart was mowing the grass in the orchard with a scythe and casting uneasy glances at the pair. Old Abe did not approve of John Osborne as a suitor for Nan. John was poor; and old Abe, although he was the wealthiest farmer in Granville, was bent on Nan's making a good match. He looked upon John Osborne as a mere fortune-hunter, and it was a thorn in the flesh to see him talking to Nan while he, old Abe, was too far away to hear what they were saying. He had a good deal of confidence in Nan; she was a sensible, level-headed girl. Still, there was no knowing what freak even a sensible girl might take into her head, and Nan was so determined when she did make up her mind. She was his own daughter in that.

However, old Abe need not have worried himself. It could not be said that Nan was helping John Osborne on in his wooing at all. Instead, she was teasing and snubbing him by turns.

Nan was very pretty. Moreover, Nan was well aware of the fact. She knew that the way her dark hair curled around her ears and forehead was bewitching; that her complexion was the envy of every girl in Granville; that her long lashes had a trick of drooping over very soft, dark eyes in a fashion calculated to turn masculine heads hopelessly. John Osborne knew all this too, to his cost. He had called to ask Nan to go with him to the Lone Lake picnic the next day. At this request Nan dropped her eyes and murmured that she was sorry, but he was too late – she had promised to go with somebody else. There was no need of Nan's making such a mystery about it. The somebody else was her only cousin, Ned Bennett, who had had a quarrel with his own girl; the latter lived at Lone

Lake, and Ned had coaxed Nan to go over with him and try her hand at patching matters up between him and his offended lady-love. And Nan, who was an amiable creature and tender-hearted where anybody's lover except her own was concerned, had agreed to go.

But John Osborne at once jumped to the conclusion – as Nan had very possibly meant him to do – that the mysterious somebody was Bryan Lee, and the thought was gall and wormwood to him.

"Whom are you going with?" he asked.

"That would be telling," Nan said, with maddening indifference.

"Is it Bryan Lee?" demanded John.

"It might be," said Nan reflectively, "and then again, you know, it mightn't."

John was silent; he was no match for Nan when it came to a war of words. He scowled moodily at the shining tumblers.

"Nan, I'm going out west," he said finally.

Nan stared at him with her last tumbler poised in mid-air, very much as if he had announced his intention of going to the North Pole or Equatorial Africa.

"John Osborne, are you crazy?"

"Not quite. And I'm in earnest, I can tell you that."

Nan set the glass down with a decided thud. John's curtness displeased her. He needn't suppose that it made any difference to her if he took it into his stupid head to go to Afghanistan.

"Oh!" she remarked carelessly. "Well, I suppose if you've got the western fever your case is hopeless. Would it be impertinent to inquire why you are going?"

"There's nothing else for me to do, Nan," said John. "Bryan Lee is going to foreclose the mortgage next month and I'll have to clear out. He says he can't wait any longer. I've worked hard enough and done my best to keep the old place, but it's been uphill work and I'm beaten at last."

Nan sat blankly down on the stool by the window. Her face was a study which John Osborne, watching old Abe's movements, missed.

"Well, I never!" she gasped. "John Osborne, do you mean to tell me that Bryan Lee is going to do that? How did he come to get your mortgage?"

"Bought it from old Townsend," answered John briefly. "Oh, he's within his rights, I'll admit. I've even got behind with the interest this past year. I'll go out west and begin over again."

"It's a burning shame!" said Nan violently.

John looked around in time to see two very red spots on her cheeks.

"You don't care though, Nan."

"I don't like to see anyone unjustly treated," declared Nan, "and that is what you've been. You've never had half a chance. And after the way you've slaved, too!"

"If Lee would wait a little I might do something yet, now that Aunt Alice is gone," said John bitterly. "I'm not afraid of work. But he won't; he means to take his spite out at last."

Nan hesitated.

"Surely Bryan isn't so mean as that," she stammered. "Perhaps he'll change his mind if – if –"

Osborne wheeled about with face aflame.

"Don't you say a word to him about it, Nan!" he cried. "Don't you go interceding with him for me. I've got some pride left. He can take the farm from me, and he can take you maybe, but he can't take my self-respect. I won't beg him for mercy. Don't you dare to say a word to him about it."

Nan's eyes flashed. She was offended to find her sympathy flung back in her face.

"Don't be alarmed," she said tartly. "I shan't bother myself about your concerns. I've no doubt you're able to look out for them yourself."

Osborne turned away. As he did so he saw Bryan Lee

driving up the lane. Perhaps Nan saw it too. At any rate, she leaned out of the window.

"John! John!" Osborne half turned. "You'll be up again soon, won't you?"

His face hardened. "I'll come to say goodbye before I go, of course," he answered shortly.

He came face to face with Lee at the gate, where the latter was tying his sleek chestnut to a poplar. He acknowledged his rival's condescending nod with a scowl. Lee looked after him with a satisfied smile.

"Poor beggar!" he muttered. "He feels pretty cheap, I reckon. I've spoiled his chances in this quarter. Old Abe doesn't want any poverty-stricken hangers-on about his place and Nan won't dream of taking him when she knows he hasn't a roof over his head."

He stopped for a chat with old Abe. Old Abe approved of Bryan Lee. He was a son-in-law after old Abe's heart.

Meanwhile, Nan had seated herself at the pantry window and was ostentatiously hemming towels in apparent oblivion of suitor No. 2. Nevertheless, when Bryan came up she greeted him with an unusually sweet smile and at once plunged into an animated conversation. Bryan had not come to ask her to go to the picnic – business prevented him from going. But he meant to find out if she were going with John Osborne. As Nan was serenely impervious to all hints, he was finally forced to ask her bluntly if she was going to the picnic.

Well, yes, she expected to.

Oh! Might he ask with whom?

Nan didn't know that it was a question of public interest at all.

"It isn't with that Osborne fellow, is it?" demanded Bryan incautiously.

Nan tossed her head. "Well, why not?" she asked.

"Look here, Nan," said Lee angrily, "if you're going to the picnic with John Osborne I'm surprised at you. What do you mean by encouraging him so? He's as poor as Job's turkey. I suppose you've heard that I've been compelled to foreclose the mortgage on his farm."

Nan kept her temper sweetly – a dangerous sign, had Bryan but known it.

"Yes; he was telling me so this morning," she answered slowly.

"Oh, was he? I suppose he gave me my character?"

"No; he didn't say very much about it at all. He said of course you were within your rights. But do you really mean to do it, Bryan?"

"Of course I do," said Bryan promptly. "I can't wait any longer for my money, and I'd never get it if I did. Osborne can't even pay the interest."

"It isn't because he hasn't worked hard enough, then," said Nan. "He has just slaved on that place ever since he grew up."

"Well, yes, he has worked hard in a way. But he's kind of shiftless, for all that – no manager, as you might say. Some folks would have been clear by now, but Osborne is one of those men that are bound to get behind. He hasn't got any business faculty."

"He isn't shiftless," said Nan quickly, "and it isn't his fault if he has got behind. It's all because of his care for his aunt. He has had to spend more on her doctor's bills than would have raised the mortgage. And now that she is dead and he might have a chance to pull up, you go and foreclose."

"A man must look out for Number One," said Bryan easily, admiring Nan's downcast eyes and rosy cheeks. "I haven't any spite against Osborne, but business is business, you know."

Nan opened her lips to say something but, remembering Osborne's parting injunction, she shut them again. She shot a scornful glance at Lee as he stood with his arms folded on the sill beside her.

Bryan lingered, talking small talk, until Nan announced that she must see about getting tea.

"And you won't tell me who is going to take you to the picnic?" he coaxed.

"Oh, it's Ned Bennett," said Nan indifferently.

Bryan felt relieved. He unpinned the huge cluster of violets on his coat and laid them down on the sill beside her before he went. Nan flicked them off with her fingers as she watched him cross the lawn, his own self-satisfied smile upon his face.

A WEEK LATER the Osborne homestead had passed into Bryan Lee's hands and John Osborne was staying with his cousin at Thornhope, pending his departure for the west. He had never been to see Nan since that last afternoon, but Bryan Lee haunted the Stewart place. One day he suddenly stopped coming and, although Nan was discreetly silent, in due time it came to old Abe's ears by various driblets of gossip that Nan had refused him.

Old Abe marched straightway home to Nan in a fury and demanded if this were true. Nan curtly admitted that it was. Old Abe was so much taken aback by her coolness that he asked almost meekly what was her reason for doing such a fool trick.

"Because he turned John Osborne out of house and home," returned Nan composedly. "If he hadn't done that there is no telling what might have happened. I might even have married him, because I liked him very well and it would have pleased you. At any rate, I wouldn't have married John when you were against him. Now I mean to."

Old Abe stormed furiously at this, but Nan kept so provokingly cool that he was conscious of wasting breath. He went off in a rage, but Nan did not feel particularly anxious now that the announcement was over. He would cool down, she knew. John Osborne worried her more. She didn't see clearly how she was to marry him unless he asked her, and he had studiously avoided her since the foreclosure.

But Nan did not mean to be baffled or to let her lover slip through her fingers for want of a little courage. She was not old Abe Stewart's daughter for nothing.

One day Ned Bennett dropped in and said that John Osborne would start for the west in three days. That evening Nan went up to her room and dressed herself in the prettiest dress she owned, combed her hair around her sparkling face in bewitching curls, pinned a cluster of apple blossoms at her belt, and, thus equipped, marched down in the golden sunset light to the Mill Creek Bridge. John Osborne, on his return from Thornhope half an hour later, found her there, leaning over the rail among the willows.

Nan started in well-assumed surprise and then asked him why he had not been to see her. John blushed – stammered – didn't know – had been busy. Nan cut short his halting excuses by demanding to know if he were really going away, and what he intended to do.

"I'll go out on the prairies and take up a claim," said Osborne sturdily. "Begin life over again free of debt. It'll be hard work, but I'm not afraid of that. I will succeed if it takes me years."

They walked on in silence. Nan came to the conclusion that Osborne meant to hold his peace.

"John," she said tremulously, "won't – won't you find it very lonely out there?"

"Of course – I expect that. I shall have to get used to it."

Nan grew nervous. Proposing to a man was really very dreadful.

"Wouldn't it be – nicer for you" – she faltered – "that is – it wouldn't be so lonely for you – would it – if – if you had me out there with you?"

John Osborne stopped squarely in the dusty road and looked at her. "Nan!" he exclaimed.

"Oh, if you can't take a hint!" said Nan in despair.

It was all of an hour later that a man drove past them as they loitered up the hill road in the twilight. It was Bryan Lee; he had taken from Osborne his house and land, but he had not been able to take Nan Stewart, after all.

The Wooing of Bessy

HEN Lawrence Eastman began going to see Bessy Houghton the Lynnfield people shrugged their shoulders and said he might have picked out somebody a little younger and prettier – but then, of course, Bessy was well off. A two-hundred-acre farm and a substantial bank account were worth going in for. Trust an Eastman for knowing upon which side his bread was buttered.

Lawrence was only twenty, and looked even younger, owing to his smooth, boyish face, curly hair, and half-girlish bloom. Bessy Houghton was in reality no more than twenty-five, but Lynnfield people had the impression that she was past thirty. She had always been older than her years – a quiet, reserved girl who dressed plainly and never went about with other young people. Her mother had died when Bessy was very young, and she had always kept house for her father. The responsibility made her grave and mature. When she was twenty her father died and Bessy was his sole heir. She kept the farm and took the reins of government in her own capable hands. She made a success of it too, which was more than many a man in Lynnfield had done.

Bessy had never had a lover. She had never seemed like other girls, and passed for an old maid when her contemporaries were in the flush of social success and bloom.

Mrs. Eastman, Lawrence's mother, was a widow with two sons. George, the older, was the mother's favourite, and the property had been willed to him by his father. To Lawrence had been left the few hundreds in the bank. He stayed at home and hired himself to George, thereby adding slowly to his small hoard. He had his eye on a farm in Lynnfield, but he was as yet a mere boy, and his plans for the future were very vague until he fell in love with Bessy Houghton.

In reality nobody was more surprised over this than Lawrence himself. It had certainly been the last thing in his thoughts on the dark, damp night when he had overtaken Bessy walking home alone from prayer meeting and had offered to drive her the rest of the way.

Bessy assented and got into his buggy. At first she was very silent, and Lawrence, who was a bashful lad at the best of times, felt tongue-tied and uncomfortable. But presently Bessy, pitying his evident embarrassment, began to talk to him. She could talk well, and Lawrence found himself entering easily into the spirit of her piquant speeches. He had an odd feeling that he had never known Bessy Houghton before; he had certainly never guessed that she could be such good company. She was very different from the other girls he knew, but he decided that he liked the difference.

"Are you going to the party at Baileys' tomorrow night?" he asked, as he helped her to alight at her door.

"I don't know," she answered. "I'm invited – but I'm all alone – and parties have never been very much in my line."

There was a wistful note in her voice, and Lawrence, detecting it, said hurriedly, not giving himself time to get frightened: "Oh, you'd better go to this one. And if you like I'll call around and take you."

He wondered if she would think him very presumptuous. He thought her voice sounded colder as she said: "I am afraid that it would be too much trouble for you."

"It wouldn't be any trouble at all," he stammered. "I'll be very pleased to take you."

In the end Bessy had consented to go, and the next evening Lawrence called for her in the rose-red autumn dusk.

Bessy was ready and waiting. She was dressed in what was for her unusual elegance, and Lawrence wondered why people called Bessy Houghton so plain. Her figure was strikingly symmetrical and softly curved. Her abundant, dark-brown hair, instead of being parted plainly and drawn back into a prim coil as usual, was dressed high on her head, and a creamy rose nestled amid the becoming puffs and waves. She wore black, as she usually did, but it was a lustrous black silk, simply and fashionably made, with frost-like frills of lace at her firm round throat and dainty wrists. Her cheeks were delicately flushed, and her wood-brown eyes were sparkling under her long lashes.

She offered him a half-opened bud for his coat and pinned it on for him. As he looked down at her he noticed what a sweet mouth she had – full and red, with a half child-like curve.

The fact that Lawrence Eastman took Bessy Houghton to the Baileys' party made quite a sensation at that festal scene. People nodded and winked and wondered. "An old maid and her money," said Milly Fiske spitefully. Milly, as was well known, had a liking for Lawrence herself.

Lawrence began to "go with" Bessy Houghton regularly after that. In his single-mindedness he never feared that Bessy would misjudge his motives or imagine him to be prompted by mercenary designs. He never thought of her riches himself, and it never occurred to him that she would suppose he did.

He soon realized that he loved her, and he ventured to hope timidly that she loved him in return. She was always rather reserved, but the few favours that meant nothing from other girls meant a great deal from Bessy. The evenings he spent with her in her pretty sitting-room, their moonlight drives over long, satin-smooth stretches of snowy roads, and their walks home from church and prayer meeting under the winter stars, were all so many moments of supreme happiness to Lawrence.

MATTERS HAD GONE THUS FAR before Mrs. Eastman got her eyes opened. At Mrs. Tom Bailey's quilting party an officious gossip took care to inform her that Lawrence was supposed to be crazy over Bessy Houghton, who was, of course, encouraging him simply for the sake of having someone to beau her round, and who would certainly throw him over in the end, since she knew perfectly well that it was her money he was after.

Mrs. Eastman was a proud woman and a determined one. She had always disliked Bessy Houghton, and she went home from the quilting resolved to put an instant stop to "all such nonsense" on her son's part.

"Where is Lawrie?" she asked abruptly, as she entered the small kitchen where George Eastman was lounging by the fire.

"Out in the stable grooming up Lady Grey," responded her older son sulkily. "I suppose he's gadding off to see Bessy Houghton again, the young fool that he is! Why don't you put a stop to it?"

"I am going to put a stop to it," said Mrs. Eastman grimly. "I'd have done it before if I'd known. You should have told me of it if you knew. I'm going out to see Lawrence right now."

George Eastman muttered something inaudible as the door closed behind her. He was a short, thickset man, not in the least like Lawrence, who was ten years his junior. Two years previously he had made a furtive attempt to pay court to Bessy Houghton for the sake of her wealth, and her decided repulse of his advances was a remembrance that made him grit his teeth yet. He had hated her bitterly ever since.

Lawrence was brushing his pet mare's coat until it shone like satin, and whistling "Annie Laurie" until the rafters rang. Bessy had sung it for him the night before. He could see her plainly still as she had looked then, in her gown of vivid red – a colour peculiarly becoming to her – with her favourite laces at wrist and throat and a white rose in her hair, which was dressed in the high, becoming knot she had always worn since the night he had shyly told her he liked it so.

She had played and sung many of the sweet old Scotch ballads for him, and when she had gone to the door with him he had taken both her hands in his and, emboldened by the look in her brown eyes, he had stooped and kissed her. Then he had stepped back, filled with dismay at his own audacity. But Bessy had said no word of rebuke, and only blushed hotly crimson. She must care for him, he thought happily, or else she would have been angry.

When his mother came in at the stable door her face was hard and uncompromising.

"Lawrie," she said sharply, "where are you going again tonight? You were out last night."

"Well, Mother, I promise you I wasn't in any bad company. Come now, don't quiz a fellow too close."

"You are going to dangle after Bessy Houghton again. It's time you were told what a fool you were making of yourself. She's old enough to be your mother. The whole settlement is laughing at you."

Lawrence looked as if his mother had struck him a blow in the face. A dull, purplish flush crept over his brow.

"This is some of George's work," he broke out fiercely. "He's been setting you on me, has he? Yes, he's jealous – he wanted Bessy himself, but she would not look at him. He thinks nobody knows it, but I do. Bessy marry him? It's very likely!"

"Lawrie Eastman, you are daft. George hasn't said anything to me. You surely don't imagine Bessy Houghton would marry you. And if she would, she is too old for you. Now, don't you hang around her any longer."

"I will," said Lawrence flatly. "I don't care what anybody says. You needn't worry over me. I can take care of myself."

Mrs. Eastman looked blankly at her son. He had never defied or disobeyed her in his life before. She had supposed her word would be law. Rebellion was something she had not dreamed of. Her lips tightened ominously and her eyes narrowed.

"You're a bigger fool than I took you for," she said in a voice that trembled with anger. "Bessy Houghton laughs at you everywhere. She knows you're just after her money, and she makes fun –"

"Prove it," interrupted Lawrence undauntedly. "I'm not going to put any faith in Lynnfield gossip. Prove it if you can."

"I can prove it. Maggie Hatfield told me what Bessy Houghton said to her about you. She said you were a lovesick fool, and she only went with you for a little amusement, and that if you thought you had nothing to do but marry her and hang up your hat there you'd find yourself vastly mistaken."

Possibly in her calmer moments Mrs. Eastman might have shrunk from such a deliberate falsehood, although it was said of her in Lynnfield that she was not one to stick at a lie when the truth would not serve her purpose. Moreover, she felt quite sure that Lawrence would never ask Maggie Hatfield anything about it.

Lawrence turned white to the lips. "Is that true, Mother?" he asked huskily.

"I've warned you," replied his mother, not choosing to repeat her statement. "If you go after Bessy any more you can take the consequences."

She drew her shawl about her pale, malicious face and left him with a parting glance of contempt.

"I guess that'll settle him," she thought grimly. "Bessy Houghton turned up her nose at George, but she shan't make a fool of Lawrence too."

Alone in the stable Lawrence stood staring out at the dull red ball of the winter sun with unseeing eyes. He had implicit faith in his mother, and the stab had gone straight to his heart. Bessy Houghton listened in vain that night for his well-known footfall on the verandah.

The next night Lawrence went home with Milly Fiske from prayer meeting, taking her out from a crowd of other girls under Bessy Houghton's very eyes as she came down the steps of the little church.

Bessy walked home alone. The light burned low in her sitting-room, and in the mirror over the mantel she saw her own pale face, with its tragic, pain-stricken eyes. Annie Hillis, her "help," was out. She was alone in the big house with her misery and despair.

She went dizzily upstairs to her own room and flung herself on the bed in the chill moonlight.

"It is all over," she said dully. All night she lay there, fighting with her pain. In the wan, grey morning she looked at her mirrored self with pitying scorn – at the pallid face, the lifeless features, the dispirited eyes with their bluish circles.

"What a fool I have been to imagine he could care for me!" she said bitterly. "He has only been amusing himself with my folly. And to think that I let him kiss me the other night!"

She thought of that kiss with a pitiful shame. She hated herself for the weakness that could not check her tears. Her lonely life had been brightened by the companionship of her young lover. The youth and girlhood of which fate had cheated her had come to her with love; the future had looked rosy with promise; now it had darkened with dourness and greyness.

Maggie Hatfield came that day to sew. Bessy had intended to have a dark-blue silk made up and an evening waist of pale pink cashmere. She had expected to wear the latter at a party which was to come off a fortnight later, and she had got it to please Lawrence, because he had told her that pink was his favourite colour. She would have neither it nor the silk made up now. She put them both away and instead brought out an ugly pattern of snuff-brown stuff, bought years before and never used.

"But where is your lovely pink, Bessy?" asked the dressmaker. "Aren't you going to have it for the party?"

"No, I'm not going to have it made up at all," said Bessy listlessly. "It's too gay for me. I was foolish to think it would ever suit me. This brown will do for a spring suit. It doesn't make much difference what I wear."

Maggie Hatfield, who had not been at prayer meeting the night before, and knew nothing of what had occurred, looked at her curiously, wondering what Lawrence Eastman could see in her to be as crazy about her as some people said he was. Bessy was looking her oldest and plainest just then, with her hair combed severely back from her pale, dispirited face.

"It must be her money he is after," thought the dressmaker. "She looks over thirty, and she can't pretend to be pretty. I believe she thinks a lot of him, though."

For the most part, Lynnfield people believed that Bessy had thrown Lawrence over. This opinion was borne out by his woebegone appearance. He was thin and pale; his face had lost its youthful curves and looked hard and mature. He was moody and taciturn and his speech and manner were marked by a new cynicism.

IN APRIL A WELL-TO-DO STOREKEEPER from an adjacent village began to court Bessy Houghton. He was over fifty, and had never been a handsome man in his best days, but Lynnfield oracles opined that Bessy would take him. She couldn't expect to do any better, they said, and she was looking terribly old and dowdy all at once.

In June Maggie Hatfield went to the Eastmans' to sew. The first bit of news she imparted to Mrs. Eastman was that Bessy Houghton had refused Jabez Lea – at least, he didn't come to see her any more.

Mrs. Eastman twitched her thread viciously. "Bessy Houghton was born an old maid," she said sharply. "She thinks nobody is good enough for her, that is what's the matter. Lawrence got some silly boy-notion into his head last winter, but I soon put a stop to that."

"I always had an idea that Bessy thought a good deal of

Lawrence," said Maggie. "She has never been the same since he left off going with her. I was up there the morning after that prayer-meeting night people talked so much of, and she looked positively dreadful, as if she hadn't slept a wink the whole night."

"Nonsense!" said Mrs. Eastman decisively. "She would never think of taking a boy like him when she'd turned up her nose at better men. And I didn't want her for a daughter-in-law anyhow. I can't bear her. So I put my foot down in time. Lawrence sulked for a spell, of course – boy-fashion – and he's been as fractious as a spoiled baby ever since."

"Well, I dare say you're right," assented the dressmaker. "But I must say I had always imagined that Bessy had a great notion of Lawrence. Of course, she's so quiet it is hard to tell. She never says a word about herself."

There was an unsuspected listener to this conversation. Lawrence had come in from the field for a drink, and was standing in the open kitchen doorway, within easy earshot of the women's shrill tones.

He had never doubted his mother's word at any time in his life, but now he knew beyond doubt that there had been crooked work somewhere. He shrank from believing his mother untrue, yet where else could the crookedness come in?

When Mrs. Eastman had gone to the kitchen to prepare dinner, Maggie Hatfield was startled by the appearance of Lawrence at the low open window of the sitting-room.

"Mercy me, how you scared me!" she exclaimed nervously.

"Maggie," said Lawrence seriously, "I want to ask you a question. Did Bessy Houghton ever say anything to you about me or did you ever say that she did? Give me a straight answer."

The dressmaker peered at him curiously.

"No. Bessy never so much as mentioned your name to me," she said, "and I never heard that she did to anyone else. Why?"

"Thank you. That was all I wanted to know," said Lawrence, ignoring her question, and disappearing as suddenly as he had come.

That evening at moonrise he passed through the kitchen dressed in his Sunday best. His mother met him at the door.

"Where are you going?" she asked querulously.

Lawrence looked her squarely in the face with accusing eyes, before which her own quailed.

"I'm going to see Bessy Houghton, Mother," he said sternly, "and to ask her pardon for believing the lie that has kept us apart so long."

Mrs. Eastman flushed crimson and opened her lips to speak. But something in Lawrence's grave, white face silenced her. She turned away without a word, knowing in her secret soul that her youngest-born was lost to her forever.

Lawrence found Bessy in the orchard under apple trees that were pyramids of pearly bloom. She looked at him through the twilight with reproach and aloofness in her eyes. But he put out his hands and caught her reluctant ones in a masterful grasp.

"Listen to me, Bessy. Don't condemn me before you've heard me. I've been to blame for believing falsehoods about you, but I believe them no longer, and I've come to ask you to forgive me."

He told his story simply and straightforwardly. In strict justice he could not keep his mother's name out of it, but he merely said she had been mistaken. Perhaps Bessy understood none the less. She knew what Mrs. Eastman's reputation in Lynnfield was.

"You might have had a little more faith in me," she cried reproachfully.

"I know – I know. But I was beside myself with pain and wretchedness. Oh, Bessy, won't you forgive me? I love you so! If you send me away I'll go to the dogs. Forgive me, Bessy."

And she, being a woman, did forgive him.

"I've loved you from the first, Lawrence," she said, yielding to his kiss.

Miss Cordelia's Accommodation

"POOR little creatures!" said Miss Cordelia compassionately.

She meant the factory children. In her car ride from the school where she taught to the bridge that spanned the river between Pottstown, the sooty little manufacturing village on one side, and Point Pleasant, which was merely a hamlet, on the other, she had seen dozens of them, playing and quarrelling on the streets or peering wistfully out of dingy tenement windows.

"Tomorrow is Saturday," she reflected, "and they've no better place to play in than the back streets and yards. It's a shame. There's work for our philanthropists here, but they don't seem to see it. Well, I'm so sorry for them it hurts me to look at them, but I can't do anything."

Miss Cordelia sighed and then brightened up, because she realized that she was turning her back upon Pottstown for two blissful days and going to Point Pleasant, which had just one straggling, elm-shaded street hedging on old-fashioned gardens and cosy little houses and trailing off into the real country in a half-hour's walk.

Miss Cordelia lived alone in a tiny house at Point Pleasant. It was so tiny that you would have wondered how anyone could live in it.

"But it's plenty big for a little old maid like me," Miss Cordelia would have told you. "And it's my own – I'm queen there. There's solid comfort in having one spot for your own self. To be sure, if I had less land and more house it would be better."

Miss Cordelia always laughed here. It was one of her jokes. There was a four-acre field behind the house. Both had been left to her by an uncle. The field was of no use to Miss Cordelia; she didn't keep a cow and she hadn't time to make a garden. But she liked her field; when people asked her why she didn't sell it she said:

"I'm fond of it. I like to walk around in it when the grass grows long. And it may come in handy some time. Mother used to say if you kept anything seven years it would come of use. I've had my field a good bit longer than that, but maybe the time will come yet. Meanwhile I rejoice in the fact that I am a landed proprietor to the extent of four acres."

Miss Cordelia had thought of converting her field into a playground for the factory children and asking detachments of them over on Saturday afternoon. But she knew that her Point Pleasant neighbours would object to this, so that project was dropped.

When Miss Cordelia pushed open her little gate, hung crookedly in a very compact and prim spruce hedge, she stopped in amazement and said, "Well, for pity's sake!"

Cynthia Ann Flemming, who lived on the other side of the spruce hedge, now came hurrying over.

"Good evening, Cordelia. I have a letter that was left with me for you."

"But – that – horse," said Miss Cordelia, with a long breath between every word. "Where did he come from? Tied at my front door – and he's eaten the tops off every one of my geraniums! Where's his owner or rider or something?"

The horse in question was a mild-eyed, rather good-looking quadruped, tied by a halter to the elm at Miss Cordelia's door and contentedly munching a mouthful of geranium stalks. Cynthia Ann came through the hedge with the letter.

"Maybe this will explain," she said. "Same boy brought it as brought the horse – a little freckly chap mostly all grin and shirtsleeves. Said he was told to take the letter and horse to Miss Cordelia Herry, Elm Street, Point Pleasant, and he couldn't wait. So he tied the creature in there and left the letter with me. He came half an hour ago. Well, he has played havoc with your geraniums and no mistake."

Miss Cordelia opened and read her letter. When she finished it she looked at the curious Cynthia Ann solemnly.

"Well, if that isn't John Drew all over! I suspected he was at the bottom of it as soon as I laid my eyes on that animal. John Drew is a cousin of mine. He's been living out at Poplar Valley and he writes me that he has gone out west, and wants me to take 'old Nap.' I suppose that is the horse. He says that Nap is getting old and not much use for work and he couldn't bear the thought of shooting him or selling him to someone who might ill-treat him, so he wants me to take him and be kind to him for old times' sake. John and I were just like brother and sister when we were children. If this isn't like him nothing ever was. He was always doing odd things and thinking they were all right. And now he's off west and here is the horse. If it were a cat or a dog – but a horse!"

"Your four-acre field will come in handy now," said Cynthia Ann jestingly.

"So it will." Miss Cordelia spoke absently. "The very thing! Yes, I'll put him in there."

"But you don't really mean that you're going to keep the horse, are you?" protested Cynthia Ann. "Why, he is no good to you – and think of the expense of feeding him!"

"I'll keep him for a while," said Miss Cordelia briskly. "As you say, there is the four-acre field. It will keep him in eating for a while. I always knew that field had a mission. Poor John Drew! I'd like to oblige him for old times' sake, as he says, although this is as crazy as anything he ever did. But I have a plan. Meanwhile, I can't feed Nap on geraniums."

Miss Cordelia always adapted herself quickly and calmly to new circumstances. "It is never any use to get in a stew about things," she was wont to say. So now she untied Nap gingerly, with many rueful glances at her geraniums, and led him away to the field behind the house, where she tied him safely to a post with such an abundance of knots that there was small fear of his getting away.

When the mystified Cynthia Ann had returned home Miss Cordelia set about getting her tea and thinking over the plan that had come to her concerning her white elephant.

"I can keep him for the summer," she said. "I'll have to dispose of him in the fall for I've no place to keep him in, and anyway I couldn't afford to feed him. I'll see if I can borrow Mr. Griggs's express wagon for Saturday afternoons, and if I can those poor factory children in my grade shall have a weekly treat or my name is not Cordelia Herry. I'm not so sure but that John Drew has done a good thing after all. Poor John! He always did take things so for granted."

ALL THE POINT PLEASANT PEOPLE soon knew about Miss Cordelia's questionable windfall, and she was overwhelmed with advice and suggestions. She listened to all tranquilly and then placidly followed her own way. Mr. Griggs was very obliging in regard to his old express wagon, and the next Saturday Point Pleasant was treated to a mild sensation – nothing less than Miss Cordelia rattling through the village, enthroned on the high seat of Mr. Griggs's yellow express wagon, drawn by old Nap who, after a week of browsing idleness in the four-acre field, was quite frisky and went at a decided amble down Elm Street and across the bridge. The long wagon had been filled up with board seats, and when Miss Cordelia came back over the bridge the boards were crowded with factory children – pale-faced little creatures whose eyes were aglow with pleasure at this unexpected outing.

Miss Cordelia drove straight out to the big pine-clad hills of Deepdale, six miles from Pottstown. Then she tied Nap in a convenient lane and turned the children loose to revel in the woods and fields. How they did enjoy themselves! And how Miss Cordelia enjoyed seeing them enjoy themselves!

When dinner time came she gathered them all around her and went to the wagon. In it she had a basket of bread and butter.

"I can't afford anything more," she told Cynthia Ann, "but they must have something to stay their little stomachs. And I can get some water at a farmhouse."

Miss Cordelia had had her eye on a certain farmhouse all the morning. She did not know anything about the people who lived there, but she liked the looks of the place. It was a big, white, green-shuttered house, throned in wide-spreading orchards, with a green sweep of velvety lawn in front.

To this Miss Cordelia took her way, surrounded by her small passengers, and they all trooped into the great farmhouse yard just as a big man stepped out of a nearby barn. As he approached, Miss Cordelia thought she had never seen anybody so much like an incarnate smile before. Smiles of all kinds seemed literally to riot over his ruddy face and in and out of his eyes and around the corners of his mouth.

"Well, well, well!" he said, when he came near enough to be heard. "Is this a runaway school, ma'am?"

"I'm the runaway schoolma'am," responded Miss Cordelia with a twinkle. "And these are a lot of factory children I've brought out for a Saturday treat. I thought I might get some water from your well, and maybe you will lend us a tin dipper or two?"

"Water? Tut, tut!" said the big man, with three distinct smiles on his face. "Milk's the thing, ma'am – milk. I'll tell my housekeeper to bring some out. And all of you come over to the lawn and make yourselves at home. Bless you, ma'am, I'm fond of children. My name is Smiles, ma'am – Abraham Smiles."

"It suits you," said Miss Cordelia emphatically, before she thought, and then blushed rosy-red over her bluntness.

Mr. Smiles laughed. "Yes, I guess I always have an everlasting grin on. Had to live up to my name, you see, in spite of my naturally cantankerous disposition. But come this way, ma'am, I can see the hunger sticking out of those youngsters' eyes. We'll have a sort of impromptu picnic here and now. I'll tell my housekeeper to send out some jam too."

While the children devoured their lunch Miss Cordelia found herself telling Mr. Smiles all about old Nap and her little project.

"I'm going to bring out a load every fine Saturday all summer," she said. "It's all I can do. They enjoy it so, the little creatures. It's terrible to think how cramped their lives are. They just exist in soot. Some of them here never saw green fields before today."

Mr. Smiles listened and beamed and twinkled until Miss Cordelia felt almost as dazzled as if she were looking at the sun.

"Look here, ma'am, I like this plan of yours and I want to have a hand in helping it along. Bring your loads of children out here every Saturday, right here to Beechwood Farm, and turn them loose in my beech woods and upland pastures. I'll put up some swings for them and have some games, and I'll provide the refreshments also. Trouble, ma'am? No, trouble and I ain't on speaking terms. It'll be a pleasure, ma'am. I'm fond of children even if I am a grumpy cross-grained old bachelor. If you can give up your own holiday to give them a good time, surely I can do something too."

When Miss Cordelia and her brood of tired, happy little lads and lasses ambled back to town in the golden dusk she felt that the expedition had been an emphatic success. Even old Nap seemed to jog along eye-deep in satisfaction. Probably he was ruminating on the glorious afternoon he had spent in Mr. Smiles's clover pasture.

Every fine Saturday that summer Miss Cordelia took some of the factory children to the country. The Point Pleasant people nicknamed her equipage "Miss Cordelia's accommodation," and it became a mild standing joke.

As for Mr. Smiles, he proved a valuable assistant. Like Miss Cordelia, he gave his Saturdays over to the children, and high weekly revel was held at Beechwood Farm.

But when the big bronze and golden leaves began to fall in the beech woods, Miss Cordelia sorrowfully realized that the summer was over and that the weekly outings which she had enjoyed as much as the children must soon be discontinued.

"I feel so sorry," she told Mr. Smiles, "but it can't be helped. It will soon be too cold for our jaunts and of course I can't keep Nap through the winter. I hate to part with him, I've grown so fond of him, but I must."

She looked regretfully at Nap, who was nibbling Mr. Smiles's clover aftermath. He was sleek and glossy. It had been the golden summer of Nap's life.

Mr. Smiles coughed in an embarrassed fashion. Miss Cordelia looked at him and was amazed to see that not a smile was on or about his face. He looked absurdly serious.

"I want to buy Nap," he said in a sepulchral tone, "but that is not the only thing I want. I want you too, ma'am. I'm tired of being a cross old bachelor. I think I'd like to be a cross old husband, for a change. Do you think you could put up with me in that capacity, Miss Cordelia, my dear?"

Miss Cordelia gave a half gasp and then she had to laugh. "Oh, Mr. Smiles, I'll agree to anything if you'll only smile again. It seems unnatural to see you look so solemn."

The smiles at once broke loose and revelled over her wooer's face.

"Then you will come?" he said eagerly.

Half an hour later they had their plans made. At New Year's Miss Cordelia was to leave her school and sooty Pottstown and come to be mistress of Beechwood Farm.

"And look here," said Mr. Smiles. "Every fine Saturday you shall have a big, roomy sleigh and Nap, and drive into town for some children and bring them out here for their weekly treat as usual. The house is large enough to hold them, goodness knows, and if it isn't there are the barns for the overflow. This is going to be our particular pet charity all our lives, ma'am – I mean Cordelia, my dear."

"Blessings on old Nap," said Miss Cordelia with a happy light in her eyes.

"He shall live in clover for the rest of his days," added Mr. Smiles smilingly.

The Twins and a Wedding

OMETIMES Johnny and I wonder what would really have happened if we had never started for Cousin Pamelia's wedding. I think that Ted would have come back some time; but Johnny says he doesn't believe he ever would, and Johnny ought to know, because Johnny's a boy. Anyhow, he couldn't have come back for four years. However, we *did* start for the wedding and so things came out all right, and Ted said we were a pair of twin special Providences.

Johnny and I fully expected to go to Cousin Pamelia's wedding because we had always been such chums with her. And she did write to Mother to be sure and bring us, but Father and Mother didn't want to be bothered with us. That is the plain truth of the matter. They are good parents, as parents go in this world; I don't think we could have picked out much better, all things considered; but Johnny and I have always known that they never want to take us with them anywhere if they can get out of it. Uncle Fred says that it is no wonder, since we are a pair of holy terrors for getting into mischief and keeping everybody in hot water. But I think we are pretty good, considering all the temptations we have to be otherwise. And, of course, twins have just twice as many as ordinary children.

Anyway, Father and Mother said we would have to stay home with Hannah Jane. This decision came upon us, as Johnny says, like a bolt from the blue. At first we couldn't believe they were not joking. Why, we felt that we simply *had* to go to Pamelia's wedding. We had never been to a wedding in our lives and we were just aching to see what it would be like. Besides, we had written a marriage ode to Pamelia and we wanted to present it to her. Johnny was to recite it, and he had been practising it out behind the carriage-house for a week. I wrote the most of it. I can write poetry as slick as anything. Johnny helped me hunt out the rhymes. That is the hardest thing about writing poetry, it is so difficult to find rhymes. Johnny would find me a rhyme and then I would write a line to suit it, and we got on swimmingly.

When we realized that Father and Mother meant what they said we were just too miserable to live. When I went to bed that night I simply pulled the clothes over my face and howled quietly. I couldn't help it when I thought of Pamelia's white silk dress and tulle veil and flower girls and all the rest. Johnny said it was the wedding dinner *he* thought about. Boys are like that, you know.

Father and Mother went away on the early morning train, telling us to be good twins and not bother Hannah Jane. It would have been more to the point if they had told Hannah Jane not to bother us. She worries more about our bringing up than Mother does.

I was sitting on the front doorstep after they had gone when Johnny came around the corner, looking so mysterious and determined that I knew he had thought of something splendid.

"Sue," said Johnny impressively, "if you have any real sporting blood in you now is the time to show it. If you've enough grit we'll get to Pamelia's wedding after all."

"How?" I said as soon as I was able to say anything.

"We'll just *go*. We'll take the ten o'clock train. It will get to Marsden by eleven-thirty and that'll be in plenty of time. The wedding isn't until twelve."

"But we've never been on the train alone, and we've never been to Marsden at all!" I gasped.

"Oh, of course, if you're going to hatch up all sorts of difficulties!" said Johnny scornfully. "I thought you had more spunk!"

"Oh, I have, Johnny," I said eagerly. "I'm *all* spunk. And I'll do anything you'll do. But won't Father and Mother be perfectly savage?"

"Of course. But we'll be there and they can't send us home again, so we'll see the wedding. We'll be punished afterwards all right, but we'll have had the fun, don't you see?"

I saw. I went right upstairs to dress, trusting everything blindly to Johnny. I put on my best pale blue shirred silk hat and my blue organdie dress and my high-heeled slippers. Johnny whistled when he saw me, but he never said a word; there are times when Johnny is a duck.

We slipped away when Hannah Jane was feeding the hens.

"I'll buy the tickets," explained Johnny. "I've got enough money left out of my last month's allowance because I didn't waste it all on candy as you did. You'll have to pay me back when you get your next month's jink, remember. I'll ask the conductor to tell us when we get to Marsden. Uncle Fred's house isn't far from the station, and we'll be sure to know it by all the cherry trees round it."

It sounded easy, and it *was* easy. We had a jolly ride, and finally the conductor came along and said, "Here's your jumping-off place, kiddies."

Johnny didn't like being called a kiddy, but I saw the conductor's eye resting admiringly on my blue silk hat and I forgave him.

Marsden was a pretty little village, and away up the road we saw Uncle Fred's place, for it was fairly smothered in cherry trees all white with lovely bloom. We started for it as fast as we could go, for we knew we had no time to lose. It is perfectly dreadful trying to hurry when you have on high-heeled shoes, but I said nothing and just tore along, for I knew Johnny would have no sympathy for me. We finally reached the house and turned in at the open gate of the lawn. I thought everything looked very peaceful and quiet for a wedding to be under way and I had a sickening idea that it was too late and it was all over.

"Nonsense!" said Johnny, cross as a bear, because he was

really afraid of it too. "I suppose everybody is inside the house. No, there are two people over there by that bench. Let us go and ask them if this is the right place, because if it isn't we have no time to lose."

We ran across the lawn to the two people. One of them was a young lady, the very prettiest young lady I had ever seen. She was tall and stately, just like the heroine in a book, and she had lovely curly brown hair and big blue eyes and the most dazzling complexion. But she looked very cross and disdainful and I knew the minute I saw her that she had been quarrelling with the young man. He was standing in front of her and he was as handsome as a prince. But he looked angry too. Altogether, you never saw a crosser-looking couple. Just as we came up we heard the young lady say, "What you ask is ridiculous and impossible, Ted. I *can't* get married at two days' notice and I don't mean to be."

And he said, "Very well, Una, I am sorry you think so. You would not think so if you really cared anything for me. It is just as well I have found out you don't. I am going away in two days' time and I shall not return in a hurry, Una."

"I do not care if you never return," she said.

That was a fib and well I knew it. But the young man didn't – men are so stupid at times. He swung around on one foot without replying and he would have gone in another second if he had not nearly fallen over Johnny and me.

"Please, sir," said Johnny respectfully, but hurriedly. "We're looking for Mr. Frederick Murray's place. Is this it?"

"No," said the young man a little gruffly. "This is Mrs. Franklin's place. Frederick Murray lives at Marsden, ten miles away."

My heart gave a jump and then stopped beating. I know it did, although Johnny says it is impossible.

"Isn't this Marsden?" cried Johnny chokily.

"No, this is Harrowsdeane," said the young man, a little more mildly.

I couldn't help it. I was tired and warm and so disappointed. I sat right down on the rustic seat behind me and burst into tears, as the story-books say.

"Oh, don't cry, dearie," said the young lady in a very different voice from the one she had used before. She sat down beside me and put her arms around me. "We'll take you over to Marsden if you've got off at the wrong station."

"But it will be too late," I sobbed wildly. "The wedding is to be at twelve – and it's nearly that now – and oh, Johnny, I do think you might try to comfort me!"

For Johnny had stuck his hands in his pockets and turned his back squarely on me. I thought it so unkind of him. I didn't know then that it was because he was afraid he was going to cry right there before everybody, and I felt deserted by all the world.

"Tell me all about it," said the young lady.

So I told her as well as I could all about the wedding and how wild we were to see it and why we were running away to it.

"And now it's all no use," I wailed. "And we'll be punished when they find out just the same. I wouldn't mind being punished if we hadn't missed the wedding. We've never seen a wedding – and Pamelia was to wear a white silk dress – and have flower girls – and oh, my heart is just broken. I shall never get over this – never – if I live to be as old as Methuselah."

"What can we do for them?" said the young lady, looking up at the young man and smiling a little. She seemed to have forgotten that they had just quarrelled. "I can't bear to see children disappointed. I remember my own childhood too well."

"I really don't know what we can do," said the young man, smiling back, "unless we get married right here and now for their sakes. If it is a wedding they want to see and nothing else will do them, that is the only idea I can suggest."

"Nonsense!" said the young lady. But she said it as if she would rather like to be persuaded it wasn't nonsense.

I looked up at her. "Oh, if you have any notion of being married I wish you would right off," I said eagerly. "Any wedding would do just as well as Pamelia's. Please do."

The young lady laughed.

"One might just as well be married at two hours' notice as two days'," she said.

"Una," said the young man, bending towards her, "will you marry me here and now? Don't send me away alone to the other side of the world, Una."

"What on earth would Auntie say?" said Una helplessly.

"Mrs. Franklin wouldn't object if you told her you were going to be married in a balloon."

"I don't see how we could arrange – oh, Ted, it's absurd."

"'Tisn't. It's highly sensible. I'll go straight to town on my wheel for the licence and ring and I'll be back in an hour. You can be ready by that time."

For a moment Una hesitated. Then she said suddenly to me, "What is your name, dearie?"

"Sue Murray," I said, "and this is my brother, Johnny. We're twins. We've been twins for ten years."

"Well, Sue, I'm going to let you decide for me. This gentleman here, whose name is Theodore Prentice, has to start for Japan in two days and will have to remain there for four years. He received his orders only yesterday. He wants me to marry him and go with him. Now, I shall leave it to you to consent or refuse for me. Shall I marry him or shall I not?"

"Marry him, of course," said I promptly. Johnny says she knew I would say that when she left it to me.

"Very well," said Una calmly. "Ted, you may go for the necessaries. Sue, you must be my bridesmaid and Johnny shall be best man. Come, we'll go into the house and break the news to Auntie."

I never felt so interested and excited in my life. It seemed too good to be true. Una and I went into the house and there we found the sweetest, pinkest, plumpest old lady asleep in an easy-chair. Una wakened her and said, "Auntie, I'm going to be married to Mr. Prentice in an hour's time."

That was a most wonderful old lady! All she said was, "Dear me!" You'd have thought Una had simply told her she was going out for a walk.

"Ted has gone for licence and ring and minister," Una went on. "We shall be married out under the cherry trees and I'll wear my new white organdie. We shall leave for Japan in two days. These children are Sue and Johnny Murray who have come out to see a wedding – *any* wedding. Ted and I are getting married just to please them."

"Dear me!" said the old lady again. "This is rather sudden. Still – if you must. Well, I'll go and see what there is in the house to eat."

She toddled away, smiling, and Una turned to me. She was laughing, but there were tears in her eyes.

"You blessed accidents!" she said, with a little tremble in her voice. "If you hadn't happened just then Ted would have gone away in a rage and I might never have seen him again. Come now, Sue, and help me dress."

Johnny stayed in the hall and I went upstairs with Una. We had such an exciting time getting her dressed. She had the sweetest white organdie you ever saw, all frills and laces. I'm sure Pamelia's silk couldn't have been half so pretty. But she had no veil, and I felt rather disappointed about that. Then there was a knock at the door and Mrs. Franklin came in, with her arms full of something all fine and misty like a lacy cobweb.

"I've brought you my wedding veil, dearie," she said. "I wore it forty years ago. And God bless you, dearie. I can't stop a minute. The boy is killing the chickens and Bridget is getting ready to broil them. Mrs. Jenner's son across the road has just gone down to the bakery for a wedding cake."

With that she toddled off again. She was certainly a wonderful old lady. I just thought of Mother in her place. Well, Mother would simply have gone wild entirely.

When Una was dressed she looked as beautiful as a dream. The boy had finished killing the chickens, and Mrs. Franklin had sent him up with a basket of roses for us, and we had each the loveliest bouquet. Before long Ted came back with the minister, and the next thing we knew we were all standing out on the lawn under the cherry trees and Una and Ted were being married.

I was too happy to speak. I had never thought of being a bridesmaid in my wildest dreams and here I was one. How thankful I was that I had put on my blue organdie and my shirred hat! I wasn't a bit nervous and I don't believe Una was either. Mrs. Franklin stood at one side with a smudge of flour on her nose, and she had forgotten to take off her apron. Bridget and the boy watched us from the kitchen garden. It was all like a beautiful, bewildering dream. But the ceremony was horribly solemn. I am sure I shall never have the courage to go through with anything of the sort, but Johnny says I will change my mind when I grow up.

When it was all over I nudged Johnny and said "Ode" in a fierce whisper. Johnny immediately stepped out before Una and recited it. Pamelia's name was mentioned three times and of course he should have put Una in place of it, but he forgot. You can't remember everything.

"You dear funny darlings!" said Una, kissing us both. Johnny didn't like *that*, but he said he didn't mind it in a bride.

Then we had dinner, and I thought Mrs. Franklin more wonderful than ever. I couldn't have believed any woman could have got up such a spread at two hours' notice. Of course, some credit must be given to Bridget and the boy. Johnny and I were hungry enough by this time and we enjoyed that repast to the full.

We went home on the evening train. Ted and Una came to the station with us, and Una said she would write me when she got to Japan, and Ted said he would be obliged to us forever and ever.

When we got home we found Hannah Jane and Father and Mother – who had arrived there an hour before us – simply distracted. They were so glad to see us safe and sound that they didn't even scold us, and when Father heard our story he laughed until the tears came into his eyes.

"Some are born to luck, some achieve luck, and some have luck thrust upon them," he said.

Them Notorious Pigs

OHN Harrington was a woman-hater, or thought that he was, which amounts to the same thing. He was forty-five and, having been handsome in his youth, was a fine-looking man still. He had a remarkably good farm and was a remarkably good farmer. He also had a garden which was the pride and delight of his heart or, at least, it was before Mrs. Hayden's pigs got into it.

Sarah King, Harrington's aunt and housekeeper, was deaf and crabbed, and very few visitors ever came to the house. This suited Harrington. He was a good citizen and did his duty by the community, but his bump of sociability was undeveloped. He was also a contented man, looking after his farm, improving his stock, and experimenting with new bulbs in undisturbed serenity. This, however, was all too good to last. A man is bound to have some troubles in this life, and Harrington's were near their beginning when Perry Hayden bought the adjoining farm from the heirs of Shakespeare Ely, deceased, and moved in.

To be sure, Perry Hayden, poor fellow, did not bother Harrington much, for he died of pneumonia a month after he came there, but his widow carried on the farm with the assistance of a lank hired boy. Her own children, Charles and Theodore, commonly known as Bobbles and Ted, were as yet little more than babies.

The real trouble began when Mary Hayden's pigs, fourteen in number and of half-grown voracity, got into Harrington's garden. A railing, a fir grove, and an apple orchard separated the two establishments, but these failed to keep the pigs within bounds.

Harrington had just got his garden planted for the season, and to go out one morning and find a horde of enterprising porkers rooting about in it was, to put it mildly, trying. He was angry, but as it was a first offence he drove the pigs out with tolerable calmness, mended the fence, and spent the rest of the day repairing damages.

Three days later the pigs got in again. Harrington relieved his mind by some scathing reflections on women who tried to run farms. Then he sent Mordecai, his hired man, over to the Hayden place to ask Mrs. Hayden if she would be kind enough to keep her pigs out of his garden. Mrs. Hayden sent back word that she was very sorry and would not let it occur again. Nobody, not even John Harrington, could doubt that she meant what she said. But she had reckoned without the pigs. They had not forgotten the flavour of Egyptian fleshpots as represented by the succulent young shoots in the Harrington domains. A week later Mordecai came in and told Harrington that "them notorious pigs" were in his garden again.

There is a limit to everyone's patience. Harrington left Mordecai to drive them out, while he put on his hat and stalked over to the Haydens' place. Ted and Bobbles were playing at marbles in the lane and ran when they saw him coming. He got close up to the little low house among the apple trees before Mordecai appeared in the yard, driving the pigs around the barn. Mrs. Hayden was sitting on her doorstep, paring her dinner potatoes, and stood up hastily when she saw her visitor.

Harrington had never seen his neighbour at close quarters before. Now he could not help seeing that she was a very pretty little woman, with wistful, dark blue eyes and an appealing expression. Mary Hayden had been next to a beauty in her girlhood, and she had a good deal of her bloom left yet, although hard work and worry were doing their best to rob her of it. But John Harrington was an angry man and did not care whether the woman in question was pretty or not. Her pigs had rooted up his garden – that fact filled his mind.

"Mrs. Hayden, those pigs of yours have been in my garden again. I simply can't put up with this any longer. Why in the name of reason don't you look after your animals better? If I find them in again I'll set my dog on them, I give you fair warning."

A faint colour had crept into Mary Hayden's soft, milky-white cheeks during this tirade, and her voice trembled as she said, "I'm very sorry, Mr. Harrington. I suppose Bobbles forgot to shut the gate of their pen again this morning. He is so forgetful."

"I'd lengthen his memory, then, if I were you," returned Harrington grimly, supposing that Bobbles was the hired man. "I'm not going to have my garden ruined just because he happens to be forgetful. I am speaking my mind plainly, madam. If you can't keep your stock from being a nuisance to other people you ought not to try to run a farm at all."

Then did Mrs. Hayden sit down upon the doorstep and burst into tears. Harrington felt, as Sarah King would have expressed it, "every which way at once." Here was a nice mess! What a nuisance women were – worse than the pigs!

"Oh, don't cry, Mrs. Hayden," he said awkwardly. "I didn't mean – well, I suppose I spoke too strongly. Of course I know you didn't mean to let the pigs in. There, do stop crying! I beg your pardon if I've hurt your feelings."

"Oh, it isn't that," sobbed Mrs. Hayden, wiping away her tears. "It's only – I've tried so hard – and everything seems to go wrong. I make such mistakes. As for your garden, sir, I'll pay for the damage my pigs have done if you'll let me know what it comes to."

She sobbed again and caught her breath like a grieved child. Harrington felt like a brute. He had a queer notion that if he put his arm around her and told her not to worry over things women were not created to attend to he would be expressing his feelings better than in any other way. But of course he couldn't do that. Instead, he muttered that the damage didn't amount to much after all, and he hoped she wouldn't mind what he said, and then he got himself away and strode through the orchard like a man in a desperate hurry.

Mordecai had gone home and the pigs were not to be seen, but a chubby little face peeped at him from between two scrub, bloom-white cherry trees.

"G'way, you bad man!" said Bobbles vindictively. "G'way! You made my mommer cry – I saw you. I'm only Bobbles now, but when I grow up I'll be Charles Henry Hayden and you won't dare to make my mommer cry then."

Harrington smiled grimly. "So you're the lad who forgets to shut the pigpen gate, are you? Come out here and let me see you. Who is in there with you?"

"Ted is. He's littler than me. But I won't come out. I don't like you. G'way home."

Harrington obeyed. He went home and to work in his garden. But work as hard as he would, he could not forget Mary Hayden's grieved face.

"I was a brute!" he thought. "Why couldn't I have mentioned the matter gently? I daresay she has enough to trouble her. Confound those pigs!"

AFTER THAT THERE WAS A TIME OF CALM. Evidently something had been done to Bobbles' memory or perhaps Mrs. Hayden attended to the gate herself. At all events the pigs were not seen and Harrington's garden blossomed like the rose. But Harrington himself was in a bad state.

For one thing, wherever he looked he saw the mental picture of his neighbour's tired, sweet face and the tears in her blue eyes. The original he never saw, which only made matters worse. He wondered what opinion she had of him and decided that she must think him a cross old bear. This worried him. He wished the pigs would break in again so that he might have a chance to show how forbearing he could be.

One day he gathered a nice mess of tender young greens

and sent them over to Mrs. Hayden by Mordecai. At first he had thought of sending her some flowers, but that seemed silly, and besides, Mordecai and flowers were incongruous. Mrs. Hayden sent back a very pretty message of thanks, whereat Harrington looked radiant and Mordecai, who could see through a stone wall as well as most people, went out to the barn and chuckled.

"Ef the little widder hain't caught him! Who'd a-thought it?"

The next day one adventurous pig found its way alone into the Harrington garden. Harrington saw it get in and at the same moment he saw Mrs. Hayden running through her orchard. She was in his yard by the time he got out.

Her sunbonnet had fallen back and some loose tendrils of her auburn hair were curling around her forehead. Her cheeks were so pink and her eyes so bright from running that she looked almost girlish.

"Oh, Mr. Harrington," she said breathlessly, "that pet pig of Bobbles' is in your garden again. He only got in this minute. I saw him coming and I ran right after him."

"He's there, all right," said Harrington cheerfully, "but I'll get him out in a jiffy. Don't tire yourself. Won't you go into the house and rest while I drive him around?"

Mrs. Hayden, however, was determined to help and they both went around to the garden, set the gate open, and tried to drive the pig out. But Harrington was not thinking about pigs, and Mrs. Hayden did not know quite so much about driving them as Mordecai did; as a consequence they did not make much headway. In her excitement Mrs. Hayden ran over beds and whatever came in her way, and Harrington, in order to keep near her, ran after her. Between them they spoiled things about as much as a whole drove of pigs would have done.

But at last the pig grew tired of the fun, bolted out of the gate, and ran across the yard to his own place. Mrs. Hayden followed slowly and Harrington walked beside her.

"Those pigs are all to be shut up tomorrow," she said. "Hiram has been fixing up a place for them in his spare moments and it is ready at last."

"Oh, I wouldn't," said Harrington hastily. "It isn't good for pigs to be shut up so young. You'd better let them run a while yet."

"No," said Mrs. Hayden decidedly. "They have almost worried me to death already. In they go tomorrow."

They were at the lane gate now, and Harrington had to open it and let her pass through. He felt quite desperate as he watched her trip up through the rows of apple trees, her blue gingham skirt brushing the lush grasses where a lacy tangle of sunbeams and shadows lay. Bobbles and Ted came running to meet her and the three, hand in hand, disappeared from sight.

Harrington went back to the house, feeling that life was flat, stale, and unprofitable. That evening at the tea table he caught himself wondering what it would be like to see Mary Hayden sitting at his table in place of Sarah King, with Bobbles and Ted on either hand. Then he found out what was the matter with him. He was in love, fathoms deep, with the blue-eyed widow!

Presumably the pigs were shut up the next day, for Harrington's garden was invaded no more. He stood it for a week and then surrendered at discretion. He filled a basket with early strawberries and went across to the Hayden place, boldly enough to all appearance, but with his heart thumping like any schoolboy's.

The front door stood hospitably open, flanked by rows of defiant red and yellow hollyhocks. Harrington paused on the step, with his hand outstretched to knock. Somewhere inside he heard a low sobbing. Forgetting all about knocking, he stepped softly in and walked to the door of the little sitting-room. Bobbles was standing behind him in the middle of the kitchen but Harrington did not see him. He was looking at Mary Hayden, who was sitting by the table in the room with her arms flung out over it and her head bowed on them. She was crying softly in a hopeless fashion.

Harrington put down his strawberries. "Mary!" he exclaimed.

Mrs. Hayden straightened herself up with a start and looked at him, her lips quivering and her eyes full of tears.

"What is the matter?" said Harrington anxiously. "Is anything wrong?"

"Oh, nothing much," said Mrs. Hayden, trying to recover herself. "Yes, there is too. But it is very foolish of me to be going on like this. I didn't know anyone was near. And I was feeling so discouraged. The colt broke his leg in the swamp pasture today and Hiram had to shoot him. It was Ted's colt. But there, there is no use in crying over it."

And by way of proving this, the poor, tired, overburdened little woman began to cry again. She was past caring whether Harrington saw her or not.

The woman-hater was so distressed that he forgot to be nervous. He sat down and put his arm around her and spoke out what was in his mind without further parley.

"Don't cry, Mary. Listen to me. You were never meant to run a farm and be killed with worry. You ought to be looked after and petted. I want you to marry me and then everything will be all right. I've loved you ever since that day I came over here and made you cry. Do you think you can like me a little, Mary?"

It may be that Mrs. Hayden was not very much surprised, because Harrington's face had been like an open book the day they chased the pig out of the garden together. As for what she said, perhaps Bobbles, who was surreptitiously gorging himself on Harrington's strawberries, may tell you, but I certainly shall not.

The little brown house among the apple trees is shut up now and the boundary fence belongs to ancient history. Sarah King has gone also and Mrs. John Harrington reigns royally in her place. Bobbles and Ted have a small, blue-eyed, much-spoiled sister, and there is a pig on the estate who may die of old age, but will never meet his doom otherwise. It is Bobbles' pig and one of the famous fourteen.

Mordecai still shambles around and worships Mrs. Harrington. The garden is the same as of yore, but the house is a different place and Harrington is a different man. And Mordecai will tell you with a chuckle, "It was them notorious pigs as did it all."

The Dissipation of Miss Ponsonby

E HADN'T been very long in Glenboro before we managed to get acquainted with Miss Ponsonby. It did not come about in the ordinary course of receiving and returning calls, for Miss Ponsonby never called on anybody; neither did we meet her at any of the Glenboro social functions, for Miss Ponsonby never went anywhere except to church, and very seldom there. Her father wouldn't let her. No, it simply happened because her window was right across the alleyway from ours. The Ponsonby house was next to us, on the right, and between us were only a fence, a hedge of box, and a sprawly acacia tree that shaded Miss Ponsonby's window, where she always sat sewing – patchwork, as I'm alive – when she wasn't working around the house. Patchwork seemed to be Miss Ponsonby's sole and only dissipation of any kind.

We guessed her age to be forty-five at least, but we found out afterward that we were mistaken. She was only thirty-five. She was tall and thin and pale, one of those drab-tinted persons who look as if they had never felt a rosy emotion in their lives. She had any amount of silky, fawn-coloured hair, always combed straight back from her face, and pinned in a big, tight bun just above her neck – the last style in the world for any woman with Miss Ponsonby's nose to adopt. But then I doubt if Miss Ponsonby had any idea what her nose was really like. I don't believe she ever looked at herself critically in a mirror in her life. Her features were rather nice, and her expression tamely sweet; her eyes were big, timid, china-blue orbs that looked as if she had been badly scared when she was little and had never got over it; she never wore anything but black, and, to crown all, her first name was Alicia.

Miss Ponsonby sat and sewed at her window for hours at a time, but she never looked our way, partly, I suppose, from habit induced by modesty, since the former occupants of our room had been two gay young bachelors, whose names Jerry and I found out all over our window-panes with a diamond.

Jerry and I sat a great deal at ours, laughing and talking, but Miss Ponsonby never lifted her head or eyes. Jerry couldn't stand it long; she declared it got on her nerves; besides, she felt sorry to see a fellow creature wasting so many precious moments of a fleeting lifetime at patchwork. So one afternoon she hailed Miss Ponsonby with a cheerful "hello," and Miss Ponsonby actually looked over and said "good afternoon," as prim as an eighteen-hundred-and-forty fashion plate.

Then Jerry, whose name is Geraldine only in the family Bible, talked to her about the weather. Jerry can talk interestingly about anything. In five minutes she had performed a miracle – she had made Miss Ponsonby laugh. In five minutes more she was leaning half out of the window showing Miss Ponsonby a new, white, fluffy, frivolous, chiffony waist of hers, and Miss Ponsonby was leaning halfway out of hers looking at it eagerly. At the end of a quarter of an hour they were exchanging confidences about their favourite books. Jerry was a confirmed Kiplingomaniac, but Miss Ponsonby adored Laura Jean Libbey. She said sorrowfully she supposed she ought not to read novels at all since her father disapproved. We found out later on that Mr. Ponsonby's way of expressing disapproval was to burn any he got hold of, and storm at his daughter about them like the confirmed old crank he was. Poor Miss Ponsonby had to keep her Laura Jeans locked up in her trunk, and it wasn't often she got a new one.

From that day dated our friendship with Miss Ponsonby, a curious friendship, only carried on from window to window. We never saw Miss Ponsonby anywhere else; we asked her to come over but she said her father didn't allow her to visit anybody. Miss Ponsonby was one of those meek women who are ruled by whomsoever happens to be nearest them, and woe be unto them if that nearest happen to be a tyrant. Her meekness fairly infuriated Jerry.

But we liked Miss Ponsonby and we pitied her. She confided to us that she was very lonely and that she wrote poetry. We never asked to see the poetry, although I think she would have liked to show it. But, as Jerry says, there are limits.

We told Miss Ponsonby all about our dances and picnics and beaus and pretty dresses; she was never tired of hearing of them; we smuggled new library novels – Jerry got our cook to buy them – and boxes of chocolates, from our window to hers; we sat there on moonlit nights and communed with her while other girls down the street were entertaining callers on their verandahs; we did everything we could for her except to call her Alicia, although she begged us to do so. But it never came easily to our tongues; we thought she must have been born and christened Miss Ponsonby; "Alicia" was something her mother could only have dreamed about her.

We thought we knew all about Miss Ponsonby's past; but even pale, drab, china-blue women can have their secrets and keep them. It was a full half year before we discovered Miss Ponsonby's.

IN OCTOBER, Stephen Shaw came home from the west to visit his father and mother after an absence of fifteen years. Jerry and I met him at a party at his brother-in-law's. We knew he was a bachelor of forty-five or so and had made heaps of money in the lumber business, so we expected to find him short and round and bald, with bulgy blue eyes and a double chin. On the contrary, he was a tall, handsome man with clear-cut features, laughing black eyes like a boy's, and iron-grey hair. That iron-grey hair nearly finished Jerry; she thinks there is nothing so distinguished and she had the escape of her life from falling in love with Stephen Shaw.

He was as gay as the youngest, danced splendidly, went everywhere, and took all the Glenboro girls about impartially. It was rumoured that he had come east to look for a wife but he didn't seem to be in any particular hurry to find her.

One evening he called on Jerry; that is to say, he did ask for both of us, but within ten minutes Jerry had him mewed up in the cosy corner to the exclusion of all the rest of the world. I felt that I was a huge crowd, so I obligingly decamped upstairs and sat down by my window to "muse," as Miss Ponsonby would have said.

It was a glorious moonlight night, with just a hint of October frost in the air – enough to give sparkle and tang. After a few moments I became aware that Miss Ponsonby was also "musing" at her window in the shadow of the acacia tree. In that dim light she looked quite pretty. It was suddenly borne in upon me for the first time that, when Miss Ponsonby was young, she must have been very pretty, with that delicate elusive fashion of beauty which fades so early if the life is not kept in it by love and tenderness. It seemed odd, somehow, to think of Miss Ponsonby as young and pretty. She seemed so essentially middle-aged and faded.

"Lovely night, Miss Ponsonby," I said brilliantly.

"A very beautiful night, dear Elizabeth," answered Miss Ponsonby in that tired little voice of hers that always seemed as drab-coloured as the rest of her.

"I'm mopy," I said frankly. "Jerry has concentrated herself on Stephen Shaw for the evening and I'm left on the fringe of things."

Miss Ponsonby didn't say anything for a few moments. When she spoke some strange and curious note had come into her voice, as if a chord, long unswept and silent, had been suddenly thrilled by a passing hand.

"Did I understand you to say that Geraldine was – entertaining Stephen Shaw?"

"Yes. He's home from the west and he's delightful," I replied. "All the Glenboro girls are quite crazy over him. Jerry and I are as bad as the rest. He isn't at all young but he's very fascinating."

"Stephen Shaw!" repeated Miss Ponsonby faintly. "So Stephen Shaw is home again!"

"Why, I suppose you would know him long ago," I said, remembering that Stephen Shaw's youth must have been contemporaneous with Miss Ponsonby's.

"Yes, I used to know him," said Miss Ponsonby very slowly.

She did not say anything more, which I thought a little odd, for she was generally full of mild curiosity about all strangers and sojourners in Glenboro. Presently she got up and went away from her window. Deserted even by Miss Ponsonby, I went grumpily to bed.

Then Mrs. George Hubbard gave a big dance. Jerry and I were pleasantly excited. The Hubbards were the smartest of the Glenboro smart set and their entertainments were always quite brilliant affairs for a small country village like ours. This party was professedly given in honour of Stephen Shaw, who was to leave for the west again in a week's time.

On the evening of the party Jerry and I went to our room to dress. And there, across at her window in the twilight, sat Miss Ponsonby, crying. I had never seen Miss Ponsonby cry before.

"What is the matter?" I called out softly and anxiously.

"Oh, nothing," sobbed Miss Ponsonby, "only – only – I'm invited to the party tonight – Susan Hubbard is my cousin, you know – and I would like so much to go."

"Then why don't you?" said Jerry briskly.

"My father won't let me," said Miss Ponsonby, swallowing a sob as if she were a little girl of ten years old. Jerry had to dodge behind the curtain to hide a smile.

"It's too bad," I said sympathetically, but wondering a

little why Miss Ponsonby seemed so worked up about it. I knew she had sometimes been invited out before and had not been allowed to go, but she had never cared apparently.

"Well, what is to be done?" I whispered to Jerry.

"Take Miss Ponsonby to the party with us, of course," said Jerry, popping out from behind the curtain.

I didn't ask her if she expected to fly through the air with Miss Ponsonby, although short of that I couldn't see how the latter was to be got out of the house without her father knowing. The old gentleman had a den off the hall where he always sat in the evening and smoked fiercely, after having locked all the doors to keep the servants in. He was a delightful sort of person, that old Mr. Ponsonby.

Jerry poked her head as far as she could out of the window. "Miss Ponsonby, you are going to the dance," she said in a cautious undertone, "so don't cry any more or your eyes will be dreadfully red."

"It is impossible," said Miss Ponsonby resignedly.

"Nothing is impossible when I make up my mind," said Jerry firmly. "You must get dressed, climb down that acacia tree, and join us in our yard. It will be pitch dark in a few minutes and your father will never know."

I had a frantic vision of Miss Ponsonby scrambling down that acacia tree like an eloping damsel. But Jerry was in dead earnest, and really it was quite possible if Miss Ponsonby only thought so. I did not believe she would think so, but I was mistaken. Her thorough course in Libbey heroines and their marvellous escapades had quite prepared her to contemplate such an adventure calmly – in the abstract at least. But another obstacle presented itself.

"It's impossible," she said again, after her first flash of hope. "I haven't a fit dress to wear – I've nothing at all but my black cashmere and it is three years old."

But the more hindrances in Jerry's way when she sets out

to accomplish something the more determined and enthusiastic she becomes. I listened to her with amazement.

"I have a dress I'll lend you," she said resolutely. "And I'll go over and fix you up as soon as it's a little darker. Go now and bathe your eyes and just trust to me."

Miss Ponsonby's long habit of obedience to whatever she was told stood her in good stead now. She obeyed Jerry without another word. Jerry seized me by the waist and waltzed me around the room in an ecstasy.

"Jerry Elliott, how are you going to carry this thing through?" I demanded sternly.

"Easily enough," responded Jerry. "You know that black lace dress of mine – the one with the apricot slip. I've never worn it since I came to Glenboro, so nobody will know it's mine, and I never mean to wear it again for it's got too tight. It's a trifle old-fashioned, but that won't matter for Glenboro, and it will fit Miss Ponsonby all right. She's about my height and figure. I'm determined that poor soul shall have a dissipation for once in her life since she hankers for it. Come on now, Elizabeth. It will be a lark."

I caught Jerry's enthusiasm, and while she hunted out the box containing the black lace dress, I hastily gathered together some other odds and ends I thought might be useful – a black aigrette, a pair of black silk gloves, a spangled gauze fan, and a pair of slippers. They wouldn't have stood daylight, but they looked all right after night. As we left the room I caught up some pale pink roses on my table.

We pushed through a little gap in the privet hedge and found ourselves under the acacia tree with Miss Ponsonby peering anxiously at us from above. I wanted to shriek with laughter, the whole thing seemed so funny and unreal. Jerry, although she hasn't climbed trees since she was twelve, went up that acacia as nimbly as a pussy-cat, took the box and things from me, passed them to Miss Ponsonby, and got in at the window while I went back to my own room to dress, hoping old Mr. Ponsonby wouldn't be running out to ring the fire alarm.

In a very short time I heard Miss Ponsonby and Jerry at the opposite window, and I rushed to mine to see the sight. But Miss Ponsonby, with a red fascinator over her head and a big cape wrapped round her, slipped out of the window and down that blessed acacia tree as neatly and nimbly as if she had been accustomed to doing it for exercise every day of her life. There were possibilities in Miss Ponsonby. In two more minutes they were both safe in our room.

Then Jerry threw off Miss Ponsonby's wraps and stepped back. I know I stared until my eyes stuck out of my head. Was that Miss Ponsonby – that!

The black lace dress, with the pinkish sheen of its slip beneath, suited her slim shape to perfection and clung around her in lovely, filmy curves that made her look willowy and girlish. It was high-necked, just cut away slightly at the throat, and had great, loose, hanging frilly sleeves of lace. Jerry had shaken out her hair and piled it high on her head in satiny twists and loops, with a pompadour such as Miss Ponsonby could never have thought about. It suited her tremendously and seemed to alter the whole character of her face, giving verve and piquancy to her delicate little features. The excitement had flushed her cheeks into positive pinkness and her eyes were starry. The roses were pinned on her shoulder. Miss Ponsonby, as she stood there, was a pretty woman, with fifteen apparent birthdays the less.

"Oh, Alicia, you look just lovely!" I gasped. The name slipped out quite naturally. I never thought about it at all.

"My dear Elizabeth," she said, "it's like a dream of lost youth."

We got Jerry ready and then we started for the Hubbards', out by our back door and through our neighbour-on-the-left's lane to avoid all observation. Miss Ponsonby was breathless with terror. She was sure every footstep she heard behind her was her father's in pursuit. She almost fainted on the spot when a belated man came tearing along the street. Jerry and I breathed a sigh of devout thanksgiving when we found ourselves safely in the Hubbard parlour.

We were early, but Stephen Shaw was there before us. He came up to us at once, and just then Miss Ponsonby turned around.

"Alicia!" he said.

"How do you do, Stephen?" she said tremulously.

And there he was looking down at her with an expression on his face that none of the Glenboro girls he had been calling on had ever seen. Jerry and I just simply melted away. We can see through grindstones when there are holes in them!

We went out and sat down on the stairs.

"There's a mystery here," said Jerry, "but Miss Ponsonby shall explain it to us before we let her climb up that acacia tree tonight. Now that I come to think of it, the first night he called he asked me about her. Wanted to know if her father were the same old blustering tyrant he always was, and if we knew her at all. I'm afraid I made a little mild fun of her, and he didn't say anything more. Well, I'm awfully glad now that I didn't fall in love with him. I could have, but I wouldn't."

Miss Ponsonby's appearance at the Hubbards' party was the biggest sensation Glenboro had had for years. And in her way, she was a positive belle. She didn't dance, but all the middle-aged men, widowers, wedded, and bachelors, who had known her in her girlhood crowded around her, and she laughed and chatted as I hadn't even imagined Miss Ponsonby could laugh and chat. Jerry and I revelled in her triumph, for did we not feel that it was due to us? At last Miss Ponsonby disappeared; shortly after Jerry and I blundered into the library to fix some obstreperous hairpins, and there we found her and Stephen Shaw in the cosy corner.

There were no explanations on the road home, for Miss

Ponsonby walked behind us with Stephen Shaw in the pale, late-risen October moonshine. But when we had sneaked through the neighbour-to-the-left's lane and reached our side verandah we waited for her, and as soon as Stephen Shaw had gone we laid violent hands on Miss Ponsonby and made her 'fess up there on the dark, chilly verandah, at one o'clock in the morning.

"Miss Ponsonby," said Jerry, "before we assist you in returning to those ancestral halls of yours you've simply got to tell us what all this means."

Miss Ponsonby gave a little, shy, nervous laugh.

"Stephen Shaw and I were engaged to be married long ago," she said simply. "But Father disapproved. Stephen was poor then. And so – and so – I sent him away. What else could I do?" – for Jerry had snorted – "Father had to be obeyed. But it broke my heart. Stephen went away – he was very angry – and I have never seen him since. When Susan Hubbard invited me to the party I felt as if I must go – I must see Stephen once more. I never thought for a minute that he remembered me – or cared still . . ."

"But he does?" said Jerry breathlessly. Jerry never scruples to ask anything right out that she wants to know.

"Yes," said Miss Ponsonby softly. "Isn't it wonderful? I could hardly believe it – I am so changed. But he said tonight he had never thought of any other woman. He – he came home to see me. But when I never went anywhere, even when I must know he was home, he thought I didn't want to see him. If I hadn't gone tonight – oh, I owe it all to you two dear girls!"

"When are you to be married?" demanded that terrible Jerry.

"As soon as possible," said Miss Ponsonby. "Stephen was going away next week, but he says he will wait until I can get ready."

"Do you think your father will object this time?" I queried.

"No, I don't think so. Stephen is a rich man now, you know. That wouldn't make any difference with me – but Father is very – practical. Stephen is going to see him tomorrow."

"But what if he does object?" I persisted anxiously.

"The acacia tree will still be there," said Miss Ponsonby firmly.

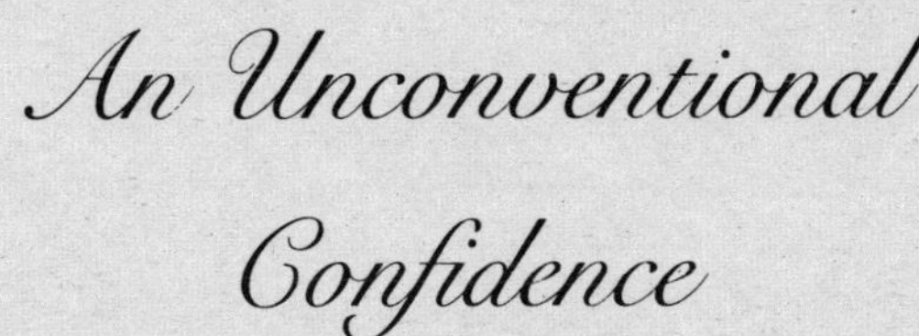
An Unconventional
Confidence

HE GIRL in Black-and-Yellow ran frantically down the grey road under the pines. There was nobody to see her, but she would have run if all Halifax had been looking on. For had she not on the loveliest new hat – a "creation" in yellow chiffon with big black *choux* – and a dress to match? And was there not a shower coming straight from the hills across the harbour?

Down at the end of the long resinous avenue the Girl saw the shore road, with the pavilion shutting out the view of the harbour's mouth. Below the pavilion, clean-shaven George's Island guarded the town like a sturdy bulldog, and beyond it were the wooded hills, already lost in a mist of rain.

"Oh, I shall be too late," moaned the Girl. But she held her hat steady with one hand and ran on. If she could only reach the pavilion in time! It was a neck-and-neck race between the rain and the Girl, but the Girl won. Just as she flew out upon the shore road, a tall Young Man came pelting down the latter, and they both dashed up the steps of the pavilion together as the rain swooped down upon them and blotted George's Island and the smoky town and the purple banks of the Eastern Passage from view.

The pavilion was small at the best of times, and just now the rain was beating into it on two sides, leaving only one dry corner. Into this the Girl moved. She was flushed and triumphant. The Young Man thought that in all his life he had never seen anyone so pretty.

"I'm so glad I didn't get my hat wet," said the Girl breathlessly, as she straightened it with a careful hand and wondered if she looked very blown and blowsy.

"It would have been a pity," admitted the Young Man. "It is a very pretty hat."

"Pretty!" The Girl looked the scorn her voice expressed. "Anyone can have a *pretty* hat. Our cook has one. This is a *creation*."

"Of course," said the Young Man humbly. "I ought to have known. But I am very stupid."

"Well, I suppose a mere man couldn't be expected to understand exactly," said the Girl graciously.

She smiled at him in a friendly fashion, and he smiled back. The Girl thought that she had never seen such lovely brown eyes before. He could not be a Haligonian. She was sure she knew all the nice young men with brown eyes in Halifax.

"Please sit down," she said plaintively. "I'm tired."

The Young Man smiled again at the idea of his sitting down because the Girl was tired. But he sat down, and so did she, on the only dry seat to be found.

"Goodness knows how long this rain will last," said the Girl, making herself comfortable and picturesque, "but I shall stay here until it clears up, if it rains for a week. I will *not* have my hat spoiled. I suppose I shouldn't have put it on. Beatrix said it was going to rain. Beatrix is such a horribly good prophet. I detest people who are good prophets, don't you?"

"I think that they are responsible for all the evils that they predict," said the Young Man solemnly.

"That is just what I told Beatrix. And I was determined to put on this hat and come out to the park today. I simply *had* to be alone, and I knew I'd be alone out here. Everybody else would be at the football game. By the way, why aren't you there?"

"I wasn't even aware that there was a football game on hand," said the Young Man, as if he knew he ought to be ashamed of his ignorance, and was.

"Dear me," said the Girl pityingly. "Where can you have been not to have heard of it? It's between the Dalhousie team and the Wanderers. Almost everybody here is on the Wanderers' side, because they are Haligonians, but I am not. I like the college boys best. Beatrix says that it is just because of my innate contrariness. Last year I simply screamed myself hoarse with enthusiasm. The Dalhousie team won the trophy."

"If you are so interested in the game, it is a wonder you didn't go to see it yourself," said the Young Man boldly.

"Well, I just couldn't," said the Girl with a sigh. "If anybody had ever told me that there would be a football game in Halifax, and that I would elect to prowl about by myself in the park instead of going to it, I'd have laughed them to scorn. Even Beatrix would never have dared to prophesy *that.* But you see it has happened. I was too crumpled up in my mind to care about football today. I had to come here and have it out with myself. That is why I put on my hat. I thought, perhaps, I might get through with my mental gymnastics in time to go to the game afterwards. But I didn't. It is just maddening, too. I got this hat and dress on purpose to wear to it. They're black and yellow, you see – the Dalhousie colours. It was my own idea. I was sure it would make a sensation. But I couldn't go to the game and take any interest in it, feeling as I do, could I, now?"

The Young Man said, of course, she couldn't. It was utterly out of the question.

The Girl smiled. Without a smile, she was charming. With a smile, she was adorable.

"I like to have my opinions bolstered up. Do you know, I want to tell you something? May I?"

"You may. I'll never tell anyone as long as I live," said the Young Man solemnly.

"I don't know you and you don't know me. That is why I want to tell you about it. I *must* tell somebody, and if I told anybody I knew, they'd tell it all over Halifax. It is dreadful to be talking to you like this. Beatrix would have three fits, one after the other, if she saw me. But Beatrix is a slave to conventionality. I glory in discarding it at times. You don't mind, do you?"

"Not at all," said the Young Man sincerely.

The Girl sighed.

"I have reached that point where I must have a confidant, or go crazy. Once I could tell things to Beatrix. That was before she got engaged. Now she tells everything to *him*. There is no earthly way of preventing her. I've tried them all. So, nowadays, when I get into trouble, I tell it out loud to myself in the glass. It's a relief, you know. But that is no good now. I want to tell it to somebody who can say things back. Will you promise to say things back?"

The Young Man assured her that he would when the proper time came.

"Very well. But please don't look at me while I'm telling you. I'll be sure to blush in places. When Beatrix wants to be particularly aggravating she says I have lost the art of blushing. But that is only her way of putting it, you know. Sometimes I blush dreadfully."

The Young Man dragged his eyes from the face under the black-and-yellow hat, and fastened them on a crooked pine tree that hung out over the bank.

"Well," began the Girl, "the root of the whole trouble is simply this. There is a young man in England. I always think of him as the Creature. He is the son of a man who was Father's especial crony in boyhood, before Father emigrated to Canada. Worse than that, he comes of a family which has contracted a vile habit of marrying into our family. It has come down through the ages so long that it has become chronic. Father left most of his musty traditions in England, but he brought this pet one with him. He and this friend agreed that the latter's son should marry one of Father's daughters. It ought to have been Beatrix – she is the oldest. But Beatrix had a pug nose. So Father settled on me. From my earliest recollection I have been given to understand that just as soon as I grew up there would be a ready-made husband imported from England for me. I was doomed to it from my cradle. Now," said the Girl, with a tragic gesture, "I ask you, could *anything* be more hopelessly, appallingly stupid and devoid of romance than that?"

The Young Man shook his head, but did not look at her.

"It's pretty bad," he admitted.

"You see," said the Girl pathetically, "the shadow of it has been over my whole life. Of course, when I was a very little girl I didn't mind it so much. It was such a long way off and lots of things might happen. The Creature might run away with some other girl – or I might have the smallpox – or Beatrix's nose might be straight when she grew up. And if Beatrix's nose were straight she'd be a great deal prettier than I am. But nothing did happen – and her nose is puggier than ever. Then when I grew up things were horrid. I never could have a single little bit of fun. And Beatrix had such a good time! She had scores of lovers in spite of her nose. To be sure, she's engaged now – and he's a horrid, faddy little creature. But he is her own choice. She wasn't told that there was a man in England whom she must marry by and by, when he got sufficiently reconciled to the idea to come and ask her. Oh, it makes me furious!"

"Is – is there – anyone else?" asked the Young Man hesitatingly.

"Oh, dear, no. How could there be? Why, you know, I couldn't have the tiniest flirtation with another man when I was as good as engaged to the Creature. That is one of my grievances. Just think how much fun I've missed! I used to rage to Beatrix about it, but she would tell me that I ought to be thankful to have the chance of making such a good match – the Creature is rich, you know, and clever. As if I cared how clever or rich he is! Beatrix made me so cross that I gave up saying anything and sulked by myself. So they think I'm quite reconciled to it, but I'm not."

"He might be very nice after all," suggested the Young Man.

"*Nice!* That isn't the point. Oh, don't you see? But no, you're a man – you *can't* understand. You must just take my word for it. The whole thing makes me furious. But I haven't told you the worst. The Creature is on his way out to Canada now. He may arrive here at any minute. And they are all so aggravatingly delighted over it."

"What do you suppose *he* feels like?" asked the Young Man reflectively.

"Well," said the Girl frankly, "I've been too much taken up with my own feelings to worry about his. But I daresay they are pretty much like mine. He must loathe and detest the very thought of me."

"Oh, I don't think he does," said the Young Man gravely.

"Don't you? Well, what do you suppose he *does* think of it all? You ought to understand the man's part of it better than I can."

"There's as much difference in men as in women," said the Young Man in an impersonal tone. "I may be right or wrong, you see, but I imagine he would feel something like this: From boyhood he has understood that away out in Canada there is a little girl growing up who is some day to be his wife. She becomes his boyish ideal of all that is good and true. He pictures her as beautiful and winsome and sweet. She is his heart's lady, and the thought of her abides with him as a safeguard and an inspiration. For her sake he resolves to make the most of himself, and live a clean, loyal life. When she comes to him she must find his heart fit to receive her. There is never a time in all his life when the dream of her does not gleam before him as of a star to which he may aspire with all reverence and love."

The Young Man stopped abruptly, and looked at the Girl. She bent forward with shining eyes, and touched his hand.

"You are splendid," she said softly. "If he thought so – but no – I am sure he doesn't. He's just coming out here like a martyr going to the stake. He knows he will be expected to propose to me when he gets here. And he knows that I know it too. And *he* knows and *I* know that I will be expected to say my very prettiest 'yes.'"

"But are you going to say it?" asked the Young Man anxiously.

The Girl leaned forward. "No. That is my secret. I am going to say a most emphatic 'no.'"

"But won't your family make an awful row?"

"Of course. But I rather enjoy a row now and then. It stirs up one's grey matter so nicely. I came out here this afternoon and thought the whole affair over from beginning to end. And I have determined to say 'no.'"

"Oh, I wouldn't make it so irreconcilable as that," said the Young Man lightly. "I'd leave a loophole of escape. You see, if you were to like him a little better than you expect, it would be awkward to have committed yourself by a rash vow to saying 'no,' wouldn't it?"

"I suppose it would," said the Girl thoughtfully, "but then, you know, I won't change my mind."

"It's just as well to be on the safe side," said the Young Man.

The Girl got up. The rain was over and the sun was coming out through the mists.

"Perhaps you are right," she said. "So I'll just resolve that I will say 'no' if I don't want to say 'yes.' That really amounts to the same thing, you know. Thank you so much for letting me tell you all about it. It must have bored you terribly, but it has done me so much good. I feel quite calm and rational now, and can go home and behave myself. Goodbye."

"Goodbye," said the Young Man gravely. He stood on the pavilion and watched the Girl out of sight beyond the pines.

When the Girl got home she was told that the Dalhousie team had won the game, eight to four. The Girl dragged her hat off and waved it joyously.

"What a shame I wasn't there! They'd have gone mad over my dress."

But the next item of information crushed her. The Creature had arrived. He had called that afternoon, and was coming to dinner that night.

"How fortunate," said the Girl, as she went to her room, "that I relieved my mind to that Young Man out in the park today. If I had come back with all that pent-up feeling seething within me and heard this news right on top of it all, I might have flown into a thousand pieces. What lovely brown eyes he had! I do dote on brown eyes. The Creature will be sure to have fishy blue ones."

WHEN THE GIRL WENT DOWN to meet the Creature she found herself confronted by the Young Man. For the first, last, and only time in her life, the Girl had not a word to say. But her family thought her confusion very natural and pretty. They really had not expected her to behave so well. As for the Young Man, his manner was flawless.

Toward the end of the dinner, when the Girl was beginning to recover herself, he turned to her.

"You know I promised never to tell," he said.

"Be sure you don't, then," said the Girl meekly.

"But aren't you glad you left the loophole?" he persisted.

The Girl smiled down into her lap.

"Perhaps," she said.

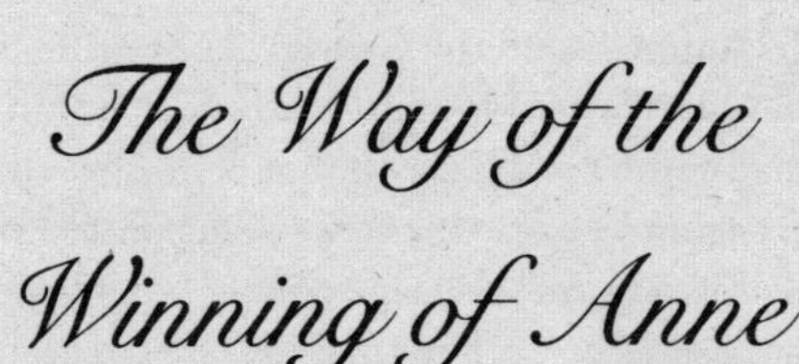
The Way of the
Winning of Anne

EROME IRVING had been courting Anne Stockard for fifteen years. He had begun when she was twenty and he was twenty-five; and now that Jerome was forty, and Anne, in a village where everybody knew everybody else's age, had to own to being thirty-five, the courtship did not seem any nearer a climax than it had at the beginning. But that was not Jerome's fault, poor fellow!

At the end of the first year he had asked Anne to marry him, and Anne had refused. Jerome was disappointed, but he kept his head and went on courting Anne just the same; that is, he went over to Esek Stockard's house every Saturday night and spent the evening, he walked home with Anne from prayer meeting and singing school and parties when she would let him, and asked her to go to all the concerts and socials and quilting frolics that came off. Anne never would go, of course, but Jerome faithfully gave her the chance. Old Esek rather favoured Jerome's suit, for Anne was the plainest of his many daughters, and no other fellow seemed at all anxious to run Jerome off the track; but she took her own way with true Stockard firmness, and matters were allowed to drift on at the will of time or chance.

Three years later Jerome tried his luck again, with precisely the same result, and after that he had asked Anne regularly once a year to marry him, and just as regularly Anne said no – a little more brusquely and a little more decidedly every year. Now, in the mellowness of a fifteen-year-old courtship, Jerome did not mind it at all. He knew that everything comes to the man who has patience to wait.

Time, of course, had not stood still with Anne and Jerome, or with the history of Deep Meadows. At the Stockard homestead the changes had been many and marked. Every year or two there had been a wedding in the big brick farmhouse, and one of old Esek's girls had been the bride each time. Julia and

Grace and Celia and Betty and Theodosia and Clementina Stockard were all married and gone. But Anne had never had another lover. There had to be an old maid in every big family, she said, and she was not going to marry Jerome Irving just for the sake of having Mrs. on her tombstone.

Old Esek and his wife had been put away in the Deep Meadows burying-ground. The broad, fertile Stockard acres passed into Anne's possession. She was a good business-woman, and the farm continued to be the best in the district. She kept two hired men and a servant girl, and the sixteen-year-old daughter of her oldest sister lived with her. There were few visitors at the Stockard place now, but Jerome "dropped in" every Saturday night with clockwork regularity and talked to Anne about her stock and advised her regarding the rotation of her crops and the setting out of her orchards. And at ten o'clock he would take his hat and cane and tell Anne to be good to herself, and go home.

Anne had long since given up trying to discourage him; she even accepted attentions from him now that she had used to refuse. He always walked home with her from evening meetings and was her partner in the games at quilting parties. It was great fun for the young folks. "Old Jerome and Anne" were a standing joke in Deep Meadows. But the older people had ceased to expect anything to come of it.

Anne laughed at Jerome as she had always done, and would not have owned for the world that she could have missed him. Jerome was useful, she admitted, and a comfortable friend; and she would have liked him well enough if he would only omit that ridiculous yearly ceremony of proposal.

It was Jerome's fortieth birthday when Anne refused him again. He realized this as he went down the road in the moonlight, and doubt and dismay began to creep into his heart. Anne and he were both getting old – there was no disputing that fact. It was high time that he brought her to terms if he was ever going to. Jerome was an easy-going mortal and always took things placidly, but he did not mean to have all those fifteen years of patient courting go for nothing. He had thought Anne would get tired of saying no, sooner or later, and say yes, if for no other reason than to have a change; but getting tired did not seem to run in the Stockard blood. She had said no that night just as coolly and decidedly and unsentimentally as she said it fifteen years before. Jerome had the sensation of going around in a circle and never getting any further on. He made up his mind that something must be done, and just as he got to the brook that divides Deep Meadows West from Deep Meadows Central an idea struck him; it was a good idea and amused him. He laughed aloud and slapped his thigh, much to the amusement of two boys who were sitting unnoticed on the railing of the bridge.

"There's old Jerome going home from seeing Anne Stockard," said one. "Wonder what on earth he's laughing at. Seems to me if I couldn't get a wife without hoeing a fifteen-year row, I'd give up trying."

But, then, the speaker was a Hamilton, and the Hamiltons never had any perseverance.

Jerome, although a well-to-do man, owning a good farm, had, so to speak, no home of his own. The old Irving homestead belonged to his older brother, who had a wife and family. Jerome lived with them and was so used to it he didn't mind.

At forty a lover must not waste time. Jerome thought out the details that night, and next day he opened the campaign. But it was not until the evening after that that Anne Stockard heard the news. It was her niece, Octavia, who told her. The latter had been having a chat up the lane with Sam Mitchell, and came in with a broad smile on her round, rosy face and a twinkle in her eyes.

"I guess you've lost your beau this time, Aunt Anne. It looks as if he meant to take you at your word at last."

"What on earth do you mean?" asked Anne, a little sharply. She was in the pantry counting eggs, and Octavia's interruption made her lose her count. "Now I can't remember whether it was six or seven dozen I said last. I shall have to count them all over again. I wish, Octavia, that you could think of something besides beaus all the time."

"Well, but listen," persisted Octavia wickedly. "Jerome Irving was at the social at the Cherry Valley parsonage last night, and he had Harriet Warren there – took her there, and drove her home again."

"I don't believe it," cried Anne, before she thought. She dropped an egg into the basket so abruptly that the shell broke.

"Oh, it's true enough. Sam Mitchell told me; he was there and saw him. Sam says he looked quite beaming, and was dressed to kill, and followed Harriet around like her shadow. I guess you won't have any more bother with him, Aunt Anne."

In the process of picking the broken egg out of the whole ones Anne had recovered her equanimity. She gave a careful little laugh.

"Well, it's to be hoped so. Goodness knows it's time he tried somebody else. Go and change your dress for milking, Octavia, and don't spend quite so much time gossiping up the lane with Sam Mitchell. He always was a fetch-and-carry. Young girls oughtn't to be so pert."

When the subdued Octavia had gone, Anne tossed the broken eggshell out of the pantry window viciously enough.

"There's no fool like an old fool. Jerome Irving always was an idiot. The idea of his going after Harriet Warren! He's old enough to be her father. And a Warren, too! I've seen the time an Irving wouldn't be seen on the same side of the road with a Warren. Well, anyhow, I don't care, and he needn't suppose I will. It will be a relief not to have him hanging around any longer."

It might have been a relief, but Anne felt strangely lonely as she walked home alone from prayer meeting the next night. Jerome had not been there. The Warrens were Methodists and Anne rightly guessed that he had gone to the Methodist prayer meeting at Cherry Valley.

"Dancing attendance on Harriet," she said to herself scornfully.

When she got home she looked at her face in the glass more critically than she had done for years. Anne Stockard at her best had never been pretty. When young she had been called "gawky." She was very tall and her figure was lank and angular. She had a long, pale face and dusky hair. Her eyes had been good – a glimmering hazel, large and long-lashed. They were pretty yet, but the crow's feet about them were plainly visible. There were brackets around her mouth too, and her cheeks were hollow. Anne suddenly realized, as she had never realized before, that she had grown old – that her youth was left far behind. She was an old maid, and Harriet Warren was young and pretty. Anne's long, thin lips suddenly quivered.

"I declare, I'm a worse fool than Jerome," she said angrily.

When Saturday night came Jerome did not. The corner of the big, old-fashioned porch where he usually sat looked bare and lonely. Anne was short with Octavia and boxed the cat's ears and raged at herself. What did she care if Jerome Irving never came again? She could have married him years ago if she had wanted to – everybody knew that!

At sunset she saw a buggy drive past her gate. Even at that distance she recognized Harriet Warren's handsome, high-coloured profile. It was Jerome's new buggy and Jerome was driving. The wheel spokes flashed in the sunlight as they crept up the hill. Perhaps they dazzled Anne's eyes a little; at least, for that or some other reason she dabbed her hand viciously over them as she turned sharply about and went upstairs. Octavia was practising her music lesson in the parlour below and singing in a sweet shrill voice. The hired men were laughing and talking in the yard. Anne slammed down her window and banged her door and then lay down on her bed; she said her head ached.

The Deep Meadows people were amused and made joking remarks to Anne, which she had to take amiably because she had no excuse for resenting them. In reality they stung her pride unendurably. When Jerome had gone she realized that she had no other intimate friend and that she was a very lonely woman whom nobody cared about. One night – it was three weeks afterward – she met Jerome and Harriet squarely. She was walking to church with Octavia, and they were driving in the opposite direction. Jerome had his new buggy and a crimson lap robe. His horse's coat shone like satin and had rosettes of crimson on his bridle. Jerome was dressed extremely well and looked quite young, with his round, ruddy, clean-shaven face and clear blue eyes.

Harriet was sitting primly and consciously by his side; she was a very handsome girl with bold eyes and was somewhat overdressed. She wore a big flowery hat and a white lace veil and looked at Anne with a supercilious smile.

Anne felt dowdy and old; she was very pale. Jerome lifted his hat and bowed pleasantly as they drove past. Suddenly Harriet laughed out. Anne did not look back, but her face crimsoned darkly. Was that girl laughing at her? She trembled with anger and a sharp, hurt feeling. When she got home that night she sat a long while by her window.

Jerome was gone – and he let Harriet Warren laugh at her – and he would never come back to her. Well, it did not matter, but she had been a fool. Only it had never occurred to her that Jerome could act so.

"If I'd thought he would I mightn't have been so sharp with him," was as far as she would let herself go even in thought.

When four weeks had elapsed Jerome came over one

Saturday night. He was fluttered and anxious, but hid it in a masterly manner.

Anne was taken by surprise. She had not thought he would ever come again, and was off her guard. He had come around the porch corner abruptly as she stood there in the dusk, and she started very perceptibly.

"Good evening, Anne," he said, easily and unblushingly.

Anne choked up. She was very angry, or thought she was. Jerome appeared not to notice her lack of welcome. He sat coolly down in his old place. His heart was beating like a hammer, but Anne did not know that.

"I suppose," she said cuttingly, "that you're on your way down to the bridge. It's almost a pity for you to waste time stopping here at all, any more than you have of late. No doubt Harriet'll be expecting you."

A gleam of satisfaction flashed over Jerome's face. He looked shrewdly at Anne, who was not looking at him, but was staring uncompromisingly out over the poppy beds. A jealous woman always gives herself away. If Anne had been indifferent she would not have given him that slap in the face.

"I dunno's she will," he replied coolly. "I didn't say for sure whether I'd be down tonight or not. It's so long since I had a chat with you I thought I'd drop in for a spell. But of course if I'm not wanted I can go where I will be."

Anne could not get back her self-control. Her nerves were "all strung up," as she would have said. She had a feeling that she was right on the brink of a "scene," but she could not help herself.

"I guess it doesn't matter much what I want," she said stonily. "At any rate, it hasn't seemed that way lately. You don't care, of course. Oh, no! Harriet Warren is all you care about. Well, I wish you joy of her."

Jerome looked puzzled, or pretended to. In reality he was hugging himself with delight.

"I don't just understand you, Anne," he said hesitatingly. "You appear to be vexed about something."

"I? Oh, no, I'm not, Mr. Irving. Of course old friends don't count now. Well, I've no doubt new ones will wear just as well."

"If it's about my going to see Harriet," said Jerome easily, "I don't see as how it can matter much to you. Goodness knows, you took enough pains to show me you didn't want me. I don't blame you. A woman has a right to please herself, and a man ought to have sense to take his answer and go. I hadn't, and that's where I made my mistake. I don't mean to pester you any more, but we can be real good friends, can't we? I'm sure I'm as much your friend as ever I was."

Now, I hold that this speech of Jerome's, delivered in a cool, matter-of-fact tone, as of a man stating a case with dispassionate fairness, was a masterpiece. It was the last cleverly executed movement of the campaign. If it failed to effect a capitulation, he was a defeated man. But it did not fail.

Anne had got to that point where an excited woman must go mad or cry. Anne cried. She sat flatly down on a chair and burst into tears.

Jerome's hat went one way and his cane another. Jerome himself sprang across the intervening space and dropped into the chair beside Anne. He caught her hand in his and threw his arm boldly around her waist.

"Goodness gracious, Anne! Do you care after all? Tell me that!"

"I don't suppose it matters to you if I do," sobbed Anne. "It hasn't seemed to matter, anyhow."

"Anne, look here! Didn't I come after you for fifteen years? It's you I always have wanted and want yet, if I can get you. I don't care a rap for Harriet Warren or anyone but you. Now that's the truth right out, Anne."

No doubt it was, and Anne was convinced of it. But she had to have her cry out – on Jerome's shoulder – and it soothed her nerves wonderfully. Later on Octavia, slipping noiselessly up the steps in the dusk, saw a sight that transfixed her with astonishment. When she recovered herself she turned and fled wildly around the house, running bump into Sam Mitchell, who was coming across the yard from a twilight conference with the hired men.

"Goodness, Tavy, what's the matter? Y' look 'sif y'd seen a ghost."

Octavia leaned up against the wall in spasms of mirth.

"Oh, Sam," she gasped, "old Jerome Irving and Aunt Anne are sitting round there in the dark on the front porch and he had his arms around her, kissing her! And they never saw nor heard me, no more'n if they were deaf and blind!"

Sam gave a tremendous whistle and then went off into a shout of laughter whose echoes reached even to the gloom of the front porch and the ears of the lovers. But they did not know he was laughing at them and would not have cared if they had. They were too happy for that.

There was a wedding that fall and Anne Stockard was the bride. When she was safely his, Jerome confessed all and was graciously forgiven.

"But it was kind of mean to Harriet," said Anne rebukingly, "to go with her and get her talked about and then drop her as you did. Don't you think so yourself, Jerome?"

Her husband's eyes twinkled.

"Well, hardly that. You see, Harriet's engaged to that Johnson fellow out west. 'Tain't generally known, but I knew it and that's why I picked on her. I thought it probable that she'd be willing enough to flirt with me for a little diversion, even if I was old. Harriet's that sort of a girl. And I made up my mind that if that didn't fetch it nothing would and I'd give up for good and all. But it did, didn't it, Anne?"

"I should say so. It was horrid of you, Jerome – but I daresay it's just as well you did or I'd likely never have found out that I couldn't get along without you. I did feel dreadful. Poor

Octavia could tell you I was as cross as X. How did you come to think of it, Jerome?"

"A fellow had to do something," said Jerome oracularly, "and I'd have done most anything to get you, Anne, that's a fact. And there it was – courting fifteen years and nothing to show for it. I dunno, though, how I did come to think of it. Guess it was a sort of inspiration. Anyhow, I've got you and that's what I set out to do in the beginning."

The Touch of Fate

RS. MAJOR HILL was in her element. This did not often happen, for in the remote prairie town of the Canadian Northwest, where her husband was stationed, there were few opportunities for matchmaking. And Mrs. Hill was – or believed herself to be – a born matchmaker.

Major Hill was in command of the detachment of Northwest Mounted Police at Dufferin Bluff. Mrs. Hill was wont to declare that it was the most forsaken place to be found in Canada or out of it; but she did her very best to brighten it up, and it is only fair to say that the N.W.M.P., officers and men, seconded her efforts.

When Violet Thayer came west to pay a long-promised visit to her old schoolfellow, Mrs. Hill's cup of happiness bubbled over. In her secret soul she vowed that Violet should never go back east unless it were post-haste to prepare a wedding trousseau. There were at least half a dozen eligibles among the M.P.s, and Mrs. Hill, after some reflection, settled on Ned Madison as the flower of the flock.

"He and Violet are simply made for each other," she told Major Hill the evening before Miss Thayer's arrival. "He has enough money and he is handsome and fascinating. And Violet is a beauty and a clever woman into the bargain. They can't help falling in love, I'm sure; it's fate!"

"Perhaps Miss Thayer may be booked elsewhere already," suggested Major Hill. He had seen more than one of his wife's card castles fall into heartbreaking ruin.

"Oh, no; Violet would have told me if that were the case. It's really quite time for her to think of settling down. She is twenty-five, you know. The men all go crazy over her, but she's dreadfully hard to please. However, she can't help liking Ned. He hasn't a single fault. I firmly believe it is foreordained."

And in this belief Mrs. Hill rested securely, but nevertheless did not fail to concoct several feminine artifices for the helping on of foreordination. It was a working belief with her that it was always well to have the gods in your debt.

Violet Thayer came, saw, and conquered. Within thirty-six hours of her arrival at Dufferin Bluff she had every one of the half-dozen eligibles at her feet, not to mention a score or more ineligibles She would have been surprised indeed had it been otherwise. Miss Thayer knew her power, and was somewhat unduly fond of exercising it. But she was a very nice girl into the bargain, and so thought one and all of the young men who frequented Mrs. Hill's drawing-room and counted it richly worth while merely to look at Miss Thayer after having seen nothing for weeks except flabby half-breed girls and blue-haired squaws.

Madison was foremost in the field, of course. Madison was really a nice fellow, and quite deserved all Mrs. Hill's encomiums. He was good-looking and well groomed – could sing and dance divinely and play the violin to perfection. The other M.P.s were all jealous of him, and more so than ever when Violet Thayer came. They did not consider that any one of them had the ghost of a chance if Madison entered the lists against them.

Violet liked Madison, and was very chummy with him after her own fashion. She thought all the M.P.s were nice boys, and they amused her, for which she was grateful. She had expected Dufferin Bluff to be very dull, and doubtless it would pall after a time, but for a change it was delightful.

The sixth evening after her arrival found Mrs. Hill's room crowded, as usual, with M.P.s. Violet was looking her best in a distracting new gown – Sergeant Fox afterwards described it to a brother officer as a "stunning sort of rig between a cream and a blue and a brown"; she flirted impartially with all the members of her circle at first, but gradually narrowed down to

Ned Madison, much to the delight of Mrs. Hill, who was hovering around like a small, brilliant butterfly.

Violet was talking to Madison and watching John Spencer out of the tail of her eye. Spencer was not an M.P. He had some government post at Dufferin Bluff, and this was his first call at Lone Poplar Villa since Miss Thayer's arrival. He did not seem to be dazzled by her at all, and after his introduction had promptly retired to a corner with Major Hill, where they talked the whole evening about the trouble on the Indian reservation at Loon Lake.

Possibly this indifference piqued Miss Thayer. Possibly she considered it refreshing after the servile adulation of the M.P.s. At any rate, when all the latter were gathered about the piano singing a chorus with gusto, she shook Madison off and went over to the corner where Spencer, deserted by the Major, whose bass was wanted, was sitting in solitary state.

He looked up indifferently as Violet shimmered down on the divan beside him. Sergeant Robinson, who was watching them jealously from the corner beyond the palms, and would have given his eyes, or at least one of them, for such a favour, mentally vowed that Spencer was the dullest fellow he had ever put those useful members on.

"Don't you sing, Mr. Spencer?" asked Violet by way of beginning a conversation, as she turned her splendid eyes full upon him. Robinson would have lost his head under them, but Spencer kept his heroically.

"No," was his calmly brief reply, given without any bluntness, but with no evident intention of saying anything more.

In spite of her social experience Violet felt disconcerted.

"If he doesn't want to talk to me I won't try to make him," she thought crossly. No man had ever snubbed her so before.

Spencer listened immovably to the music for a time. Then he turned to his companion with a palpable effort to be civilly sociable.

"How do you like the west, Miss Thayer?" he said.

Violet smiled – the smile most men found dangerous.

"Very much, so far as I have seen it. There is a flavour about the life here that I like, but I dare say it would soon pall. It must be horribly lonesome here most of the time, especially in winter."

"The M.P.s are always growling that it is," returned Spencer with a slight smile. "For my own part I never find it so."

Violet decided that his smile was very becoming to him, and that she liked the way his dark hair grew over his forehead.

"I don't think I've seen you at Lone Poplar Villa before?" she said.

"No. I haven't been here for some time. I came up tonight to see the Major about the Loon Lake trouble."

"Otherwise you wouldn't have come," thought Violet. "Flattering – very!" Aloud she said, "Is it serious?"

"Oh, no. A mere squabble among the Indians. Have you ever visited the Reservation, Miss Thayer? No? Well, you should get some of your M.P. friends to take you out. It would be worth while."

"Why don't you ask me to go yourself?" said Violet audaciously.

Spencer smiled again. "Have I failed in politeness by not doing so? I fear you would find me an insufferably dull companion."

So he was not going to ask her after all. Violet felt piqued. She was also conscious of a sensation very near akin to disappointment. She looked across at Madison. How trim and dapper he was!

"I hate a bandbox man," she said to herself.

Spencer meanwhile had picked up one of Mrs. Hill's novels from the stand beside him.

"*Fools of Habit*," he said, glancing at the cover. "I see it is making quite a sensation down east. I suppose you've read it?"

"Yes. It is very frivolous and clever – all froth but delightful froth. Did you like it?"

Spencer balanced the novel reflectively on his slender brown hand.

"Well, yes, rather. But I don't care for novels as a rule. I don't understand them. The hero of this book, now – do you believe that a man in love would act as he did?"

"I don't know," said Violet amusedly. "You ought to be a better judge than I. You are a man."

"I have never loved anybody, so I am in no position to decide," said Spencer.

There was as little self-consciousness in his voice as if he were telling her a fact concerning the Loon Lake trouble. Violet rose to the occasion.

"You have an interesting experience to look forward to," she said.

Spencer turned his deep-set grey eyes squarely upon her.

"I don't know that. When I said I had never loved, I meant more than the love of a man for some particular woman. I meant love in every sense. I do not know what it is to have an affection for any human being. My parents died before I can remember. My only living relative was a penurious old uncle who brought me up for shame's sake and kicked me out on the world as soon as he could. I don't make friends easily. I have a few acquaintances whom I like, but there is not a soul on earth for whom I care, or who cares for me."

"What a revelation love will be to you when it comes," said Violet softly. Again he looked into her eyes.

"Do you think it will come?" he asked.

Before she could reply Mrs. Hill pounced upon them. Violet was wanted to sing. Mr. Spencer would excuse her, wouldn't he? Mr. Spencer did so obligingly. Moreover, he got up and bade his hostess good night. Violet gave him her hand.

"You will call again?" she said.

Spencer looked across at Madison – perhaps it was accidental.

"I think not," he said. "If, as you say, love will come some time, it would be a very unpleasant revelation if it came in hopeless guise, and one never knows what may happen."

Miss Thayer was conscious of a distinct fluttering of her heart as she went across to the piano. This was a new sensation for her, and worthy of being analyzed. After the M.P.s had gone she asked Mrs. Hill who Mr. Spencer was.

"Oh, John Spencer," said Mrs. Hill carelessly. "He's at the head of the Land Office here. That's really all I know about him. Jack says he is a downright good fellow and all that, you know. But he's no earthly good in a social way; he can't talk or he won't. He's flat. So different from Mr. Madison, isn't he?"

"Very," said Violet emphatically.

After Mrs. Hill had gone out Violet walked to the nearest mirror and looked at herself with her forefinger in the dimple of her chin.

"It is very odd," she said. She did not mean the dimple.

SPENCER HAD TOLD HER he was not coming back. She did not believe this, but she did not expect him for a few days. Consequently, when he appeared the very next evening she was surprised. Madison, to whom she was talking when Spencer entered, does not know to this day what she had started to say to him, for she never finished her sentence.

"I wonder if it is the Loon Lake affair again?" she thought nervously.

Mrs. Hill came up at this point and whisked Madison off for a waltz. Spencer, seeing his chance, came straight across the room to her. Sergeant Robinson, who was watching them as usual, is willing to make affidavit that Miss Thayer changed colour.

After his greeting Spencer said nothing. He sat beside her, and they watched Mrs. Hill and Madison dancing. Violet wondered why she did not feel bored. When she saw Madison coming back to her she was conscious of an unreasonable anger with him. She got up abruptly.

"Let us go out on the verandah," she said imperiously. "It is absolutely stifling in here."

They went out. It was very cool and dusky. The lights of the town twinkled out below them, and the prairie bluffs behind them were dark and sibilant.

"I am going to drive over to Loon Lake tomorrow afternoon to look into affairs there," said Spencer. "Will you go with me?"

Violet reflected a moment. "You didn't ask me as if you really wanted me to go," she said.

Spencer put his hand over the white fingers that rested on the railing. He bent forward until his breath stirred the tendrils of hair on her forehead.

"Yes, I do," he said distinctly. "I want you to go with me to Loon Lake tomorrow more than I ever wanted anything in my life before."

Later on, when everybody had gone, Violet had her bad quarter of an hour with Mrs. Hill. That lady felt herself aggrieved.

"I think you treated poor Ned very badly tonight, Vi. He felt really blue over it. And it was awfully bad form to go out with Spencer as you did and stay there so long. And you oughtn't to flirt with him – he doesn't understand the game."

"I'm not going to flirt with him," said Miss Thayer calmly.

"Oh, I suppose it's just your way. Only don't turn the poor fellow's head. By the way, Ned is coming up with his camera tomorrow afternoon to take us all."

"I'm afraid he won't find me at home," said Violet sweetly. "I am going out to Loon Lake with Mr. Spencer."

Mrs. Hill flounced off to bed in a pet. She was disgusted with everything, she declared to the Major. Things had been going so nicely, and now they were all muddled.

"Isn't Madison coming up to time?" queried the Major sleepily.

"Madison! It's Violet. She is behaving abominably. She treated poor Ned shamefully tonight. You saw yourself how she acted with Spencer, and she's going to Loon Lake with him tomorrow, she says. I'm sure I don't know what she can see in him. He's the dullest, pokiest fellow alive – so different from her in every way."

"Perhaps that is why she likes him," suggested the Major. "The attraction of opposites and all that, you know."

But Mrs. Hill crossly told him he didn't know anything about it, so, being a wise man, he held his tongue.

DURING THE NEXT TWO WEEKS Mrs. Hill was the most dissatisfied woman in the four districts, and every M.P. down to the rawest recruit anathemized Spencer in secret a dozen times a day. Violet simply dropped everyone else, including Madison, in the coolest, most unmistakable way.

One night Spencer did not come to Lone Poplar Villa. Violet looked for him to the last. When she realized that he was not coming she went to the verandah to have it out with herself. As she sat huddled up in a dim corner beneath a silkily rustling western maple two M.P.s came out and, not seeing her, went on with their conversation.

"Heard about Spencer?" questioned one.

"No. What of him?"

"Well, they say Miss Thayer's thrown him over. Yesterday I was passing here about four in the afternoon and I saw Spencer coming in. I went down to the Land Office and was chatting to Cribson when the door opened about half an hour later and Spencer burst in. He was pale as the dead, and looked wild. 'Has Fyshe gone to Rainy River about those Crown

Lands yet?' he jerked out. Cribson said, 'No.' 'Then tell him he needn't; I'm going myself,' said Spencer and out he bolted. He posted off to Rainy River today, and won't be back for a fortnight. She'll be gone then."

"Rather rough on Spencer after the way she encouraged him," returned the other as they passed out of earshot.

Violet got up. All the callers were gone, and she swept in to Mrs. Hill dramatically.

"Edith," she said in the cold, steady voice that, to those who knew her, meant breakers ahead for somebody, "Mr. Spencer was here yesterday when I was riding with the Major, was he not? What did you tell him about me?"

Mrs. Hill looked at Violet's blazing eyes and wilted.

"I – didn't tell him anything – much."

"What was it?"

Mrs. Hill began to sob.

"Don't look at me like that, Violet! He just dropped in and we were talking about you – at least I was – and I had heard that Harry St. Maur was paying you marked attention before you came west – and – and that some people thought you were engaged – and so – and so –"

"You told Mr. Spencer that I was engaged to Harry St. Maur?"

"No-o-o – I just hinted. I didn't mean an-any harm. I never dreamed you'd really c-care. I thought you were just amusing yourself – and so did everybody – and I wanted Ned Madison –"

Violet had turned very pale.

"I love him," she said hoarsely, "and you've sent him away. He's gone to Rainy River. I shall never see him again!"

"Oh, yes, you will," gasped Mrs. Hill faintly. "He'll come back when he knows – you c-can write and tell him –"

"Do you suppose I am going to write and ask him to come back?" said Violet wildly. "I've enough pride left yet to keep me from doing that for a man at whose head I've thrown myself openly – yes, openly, and who has never, in words at least, told me he cared anything about me. I will never forgive you, Edith!"

Then Mrs. Hill found herself alone with her lacerated feelings. After soothing them with a good cry, she set to work thinking seriously. There was no doubt she had muddled things badly, but there was no use leaving them in a muddle when a word or two fitly spoken might set them straight.

Mrs. Hill sat down and wrote a very diplomatic letter before she went to bed, and the next morning she waylaid Sergeant Fox and asked him if he would ride down to Rainy River with a very important message for Mr. Spencer. Sergeant Fox wondered what it could be, but it was not his to reason why; it was his only to mount and ride with all due speed, for Mrs. Hill's whims and wishes were as stringent and binding as the rules of the force.

That evening when Mrs. Hill and Violet – the latter very silent and regal – were sitting on the verandah, a horseman came galloping up the Rainy River trail. Mrs. Hill excused herself and went in. Five minutes later John Spencer, covered with the alkali dust of his twenty miles' ride, dismounted at Violet's side.

THE M.P.S GAVE A CONCERT at the barracks that night and Mrs. Hill and her Major went to it, as well as everyone else of any importance in town except Violet and Spencer. They sat on Major Hill's verandah and watched the moon rising over the bluffs and making milk-white reflections in the prairie lakes.

"It seems a year of misery since last night," sighed Violet happily.

"You couldn't have been quite as miserable as I was," said Spencer earnestly. "You were everything – absolutely everything to me. Other men have little rills and driblets of affection for sisters and cousins and aunts, but everything in me went out to you. Do you remember you told me the first time we met that love would be a revelation to me? It has been more. It has been a new gospel. I hardly dared hope you could care for me. Even yet I don't know why you do."

"I love you," said Violet gravely, "because you are you."

Than which, of course, there could be no better reason.

What Aunt Marcella Would Have Called It

F AUNT Marcella had allowed Glen to bob her hair this story would never have been told because there would have been no story to tell. But Aunt Marcella did not approve of bobbed hair at all. It was flying in the face of Providence for a girl to bob her hair, and . . . so Aunt Marcella said . . . she would be bald in her old age for her sins.

"You will thank me when you are sixty," she told Glen.

"That is a long time to wait for gratitude," said Glen darkly.

But Aunt Marcella was adamant, and Glen continued to wear her lovely golden-brown braid hanging down her back like a twelve-year-old schoolgirl of the century's teens, when she would be eighteen in another month and every bit as modern as Aunt Marcella would let her be.

Aunt Marcella would not even allow her to put it up. It was intolerable. If she could even put her hair up in a lovely soft knot at the back of her neck . . . well, it might dawn on Dudley Wyatt's perception that she was really grown-up and not the schoolgirl, devoted to dolls, that he considered her and, as seemed likely, would go on considering her until she was that mythical sixty of Aunt Marcella's warnings.

It seemed to Glen that she had always been in love with Dudley Wyatt, although she had known him only from the age of twelve, when he had come to live next door to them at Nokomis Lodge. Glen always avowed that her legs trembled the first time she saw him, by which token she knew that she had fallen in love. But Dudley took no notice of her. He was all for Isabel. Not that he was in love with Isabel at all. To him, sixteen-year-old Isabel was just one of the two children at the Lindens. But she was a very clever child and he liked to talk to her. Nobody thought Glen had any brains because she hardly ever talked. And at twelve she had been anything but pretty . . . a gaunt, scrawny creature with two sunburned pigtails. Glen would go hatless, to Aunt Marcella's mid-Victorian horror.

"What kind of complexion will you have when you are sixty?" she asked. "Besides, I call it 'Brazen' to go about without a hat."

Aunt Marcella never pronounced an adjective without making you see it spelled with a capital.

But even at sixteen Isabel was a beauty . . . a tall, willowy thing with golden-brown hair and big owlish eyes that were the tint of a copper-grey sea. And, although Dudley Wyatt did not seem to have any kind of eyes for women at all, Glen believed in her secret soul that, if Isabel hadn't been so pretty, Dudley would not have detected her cleverness so quickly. As it was, he thought her a wonder. Aunt Marcella didn't. Aunt Marcella did not believe in a woman having brains.

"I call it 'Unwomanly' to be so clever," she told Isabel severely. "Aping the men!"

"But most men are really very stupid," said Isabel.

"I call that 'Flippant,'" said Aunt Marcella, "and I dislike flippancy above all things."

"Besides, if you are not clever you bore the men after your novelty wears off," persisted Isabel.

"I have never been a man," said Aunt Marcella superfluously, "but I think it takes some time for them to tire of beauty. And 'bore' was not considered a nice word when I was a girl."

And then Uncle Maurice's daughter had died and Uncle Maurice had come home and taken Isabel out west with him. That was five years ago and she had never been back since. But she was still tremendously clever and had graduated with the highest honours. Aunt Marcella called that very "Unfeminine," but Dudley exulted.

He wrote to Isabel occasionally and took the keenest interest in her career. He also made quite a bit of Glen, but still only as a child who was a dear little thing, rather dumb. Glen knew she was dumb when Dudley was about. She wasn't going to talk to him as a child and when she tried to talk to him as a grown-up her tongue clave to the roof of her mouth. She had a horrible feeling that if she did talk to him like a grown-up Dudley would smile kindly, as at a precocious child, and tell her to run away and tuck up her doll-babies.

Oh . . . Glen clenched her hands . . . life wasn't fair to women! Why . . . why . . . were men so blind? Couldn't he see she wasn't a child any longer? Couldn't he see the love she had to give him? It was bitter to have such a gift to give and nobody wanting to take it. Glen wouldn't have minded so much if Dudley had hated her . . . if only he hated her as a woman. She couldn't go on being regarded as a child.

"I love him, and he doesn't even know that I exist," she sighed. "He thinks me somebody who doesn't exist . . . the twelve-year-old arms-and-legs I was when he came here first. Why can't I make him see? He won't see! He looks at me with the condescending kindness one shows a child . . . and then I feel exactly like a caterpillar someone has stepped on."

That night he strolled past as she sat on the porch and called out teasingly, "Tell me what you are thinking of, Glennie?"

Good heavens, suppose she did tell him! Suppose she called back, "I'm thinking of you and how heavenly it would be if you came in here and sat down beside me and said, 'I love you, Glen,' and . . . and . . . kissed me."

Just what would happen? Well, she knew one thing that would. Aunt Marcella, by the living-room window, would die of frustration because she would not be able to find an adjective strong enough to describe such behaviour. But even then Dudley would probably only say something like, "You've mistaken me for Clark Adams."

Clark Adams! That immature creature of twenty!

"I don't care for boys . . . I get on better with men," Glen heard herself calling back.

But of course she had really said nothing when he asked her that question. He hadn't expected her to say anything. If only she could have thought of something quite daring to say! Something that a child couldn't think of saying. Isabel, now, could have said a dozen provocative things. Even she herself could have said them to Clark Adams. But she had said nothing . . . had only given a foolish little giggle . . . and Dudley had gone on, his dog slouching at his heels, on one of those long hikes of his that she longed to share. But Dudley had asked her only once and Aunt Marcella disapproved, tilting her hawk nose.

"I call it 'Unladylike' to go striding over the country like a man, or like one of those dreadful girls in knickerbockers," said Aunt Marcella. "I suppose you hardly class yourself among them, Glen."

The joke was that Glen was dying to wear knickers, or do anything else that might make Dudley realize that she was grown-up and beautiful . . . hair just as glossy and golden-brown as Isabel's, eyes just the same coppery grey, shoulders just as smooth and delicious. But of what use was it? Dudley never saw her shoulders.

When Isabel's letter came, saying that she was coming east for a visit, Glen had two reactions. The first was of delight in the thought of seeing Isabel again. The second was a horrible little fear. Dudley had always admired Isabel so much. And now Isabel was coming back, a brilliant M.A., no doubt more beautiful than ever . . . and what would happen to Dudley? Glen cried herself to sleep that night and hated herself for being so unsisterly.

Isabel stopped off in a mid-western town to see a college friend, but two of her trunks came on ahead of her. Isabel sent Glen the keys and would she please take out the dresses and hang them up? Glen did so, divided between delight in the lovely things and envious pangs over the effect they would likely have on Dudley. There was one in especial . . . the orchid chiffon with the black velvet girdle and a sort of pale blue perfume hanging about it. Glen tried to think what she would look like in it. But she did not try it on. Aunt Marcella would have called it 'Rude' to try on other people's clothes.

ON THE AFTERNOON of the day Isabel was expected a wire came saying that her friend had persuaded her to stay over for the weekend. Aunt Marcella thereupon decided to spend the weekend with her sister and departed so hurriedly to catch the only train that she had not time to give Glen half as many warnings as usual. Not that it mattered. Glen knew them all by heart.

"You'd better telephone Dudley that Isabel won't be here tonight. He was coming over to see her," said Aunt Marcella from the taxi.

Glen went in and tried to telephone. But Dudley's housekeeper said that he was out and wouldn't be home till dinner time. He was lecturing before some club on the Peaceful Adjustment of International Difficulties.

Glen ran up to her room with the intention of having a good cry. But when she got there she changed her mind.

"Crying won't do any good. The girls of Aunt Marcella's generation cried. I've got to do better than that. Now, what can I do to wake Dudley up before Isabel comes?"

Glen sat up on her bed suddenly. An idea had flashed into her mind, a breath-taking idea. Could she . . . dared she? But why not? She looked so much like Isabel when Isabel had been seventeen.

After dinner, when she had eaten nothing to speak of, Glen fled up to her room again. She brought the shimmering orchid dress from the guest-room closet and breathlessly slipped into it. It fitted her to perfection . . . and it was so beautifully long. How lucky Isabel had the new long dresses! Then she twisted her gold-brown hair into a knot at the nape of her neck . . . too big a knot to be fashionable, but Dudley wouldn't notice that. Isabel's earrings and necklace went on . . . sparkling amber beads that hung about her neck and over her dress like drops of golden dew . . . earrings long enough to reach her shoulders, sophisticated earrings which Aunt Marcella would have called "Theatrical." But Glen gave a gasp of delight when she looked in the glass. Oh, she was beautiful! And nobody would ever dream of taking her for a child. What a difference a long dress and a knot of hair made!

She met Dudley in the porch where there was only one dim shaded lamp. He took the hands . . . very cold hands . . . which she held out to him.

"And this is Isabel. I had forgotten how beautiful you were."

For once in her life Glen was frightened into being clever . . . and "Bold," as Aunt Marcella would have called it.

"I was afraid you had forgotten," she murmured. "That is why I came back . . . to make you remember."

Could she really have said such a thing . . . she, shy, tongue-tied Glen? But she wasn't Glen; she was Isabel. In putting on Isabel's dress she seemed to have put on Isabel's personality. She felt gay, daring, brilliant. And Dudley was so easily deceived. Glen felt a pang of anger because he was so easily deceived . . . because he knew her so little as to mistake her for Isabel. Her anger sent a naughty sparkle into her eyes and a rose-red flush into her cheeks. She would punish him.

"Let us sit down here . . . it's so much cooler and pleasanter than indoors . . . and just talk. We have five years to catch up with. Dudley, have they seemed as long to you as to me?"

"Longer," said Dudley briefly but eloquently. He seemed to find it impossible to take his eyes off her.

"I think I've been homesick every moment of the time I was away," murmured Glen. She made a place for Dudley on the cushions beside her and began to pat his dog, who was nuzzling her knee.

"You've been doing wonderful things," said Dudley, a

little absently, looking at the dog. "We've followed your career with pride, as the *Weekly Journal* puts it. I always knew you had it in you to win success."

"Oh . . . success!" Glen sighed and looked sidewise at him. "A girl wants more than that kind of success, Dudley. I've really been wretchedly lonely these past five years. But don't let's talk of me. I want to hear all about you, Dudley. What have you been doing . . . thinking . . . feeling?"

"Shall I tell you what I'm feeling just at present?" said Dudley, bending nearer. "I'm feeling drunk . . . just with looking at you, Isabel. There hasn't been any five years . . . time has gone back . . . we'll begin just where we left off."

"Do you really think we can?" said Glen in a low voice. She was quite furious to hear him making love so beautifully . . . to Isabel.

"I do. I realize some things now that it has taken me five years to realize. Isabel, there's going to be a moonrise in a few minutes . . . let us go out and watch it together. How long is it since we've seen a moonrise together?"

"Just two nights," cried Glen, springing up. "We watched the moon rise Thursday night. Dudley, I can't go on with this . . . I don't know what got into me. I'm not Isabel . . . I'm Glen!"

"Well, I know that," said Dudley, getting up too. "Just at first you tricked me, with that long dress and that hair. Then when Wags began nosing you . . . my suspicious Wags who wouldn't have a word to say to a stranger like Isabel – he's never seen her . . . I knew you for what you were."

"A horrid, shameless little imposter," said Glen piteously.

"The loveliest, sweetest woman I've ever seen . . . the woman I've been waiting for all my life," said Dudley. He had his arms around her now. "The woman I've never seen until my blind eyes were opened tonight. Thank heaven you're not Isabel. If you were I'd have to have some consideration for your five years' absence and not say everything I want to say tonight. As it is, we're old pals and I can say just what I like and as soon as I like. Because we're going to be new, new lovers, aren't we, Glen darling?"

"Oh!" said Glen. It was a very eloquent speech. Much more eloquent than the cleverest woman could have made. And evidently much more satisfying to Dudley.

"I'm going to tell your Aunt Marcella as soon as she comes back," he said. "She'll say you're too young to be married but don't you let her make you believe it. I've wasted enough time. And now let's go out and see that the moon rises properly."

When Glen went to her room that night she took off the orchid dress and held it to her lips.

"I'm going to ask Isabel to give me this. Oh, I think I've been quite crazy. I do wonder what Aunt Marcella would call my conduct."

Aunt Marcella would have called it entirely "Shameless" if she had ever known of it. But then she didn't.

When Jack and Jill Took a Hand

Jack's Side of It

ILL says I have to begin this story because it was me – I mean it was I – who made all the trouble in the first place. That is so like Jill. She is such a good hand at forgetting. Why, it was she who suggested the plot to me. I should never have thought of it myself – not that Jill is any smarter than I am, either, but girls are such creatures for planning up mischief and leading other folks into it and then laying the blame on them when things go wrong. How could I tell Dick would act so like a mule? I thought grown-up folks had more sense. Aunt Tommy was down on me for weeks, while she thought Jill a regular heroine. But there! Girls don't know anything about being fair, and I am determined I will never have anything more to do with them and their love affairs as long as I live. Jill says I will change my mind when I grow up, but I won't.

Still, Jill is a pretty good sort of girl. I have to scold her sometimes, but if any other chap tried to I would punch his head for him.

I suppose it *is* time I explained who Dick and Aunt Tommy are. Dick is our minister. He hasn't been it very long. He only came a year ago. I shall never forget how surprised Jill and I were that first Sunday we went to church and saw him. We had always thought that ministers had to be old. All the ministers we knew were. Mr. Grinnell, the one before Dick came, must have been as old as Methuselah. But Dick was young – and good-looking. Jill said she thought it a positive sin for a minister to be so good-looking, it didn't seem Christian; but that was just because all the ministers we knew happened to be homely so that it didn't appear natural.

Dick was tall and pale and looked as if he had heaps of brains. He had thick curly brown hair and big dark blue eyes – Jill said his eyes were like an archangel's, but how could she tell? She never saw an archangel. I liked his nose. It was so straight and finished-looking. Mr. Grinnell had the worst-looking nose you ever saw. Jill and I used to make poetry about it in church to keep from falling asleep when he preached such awful long sermons.

Dick preached great sermons. They were so nice and short. It was such fun to hear him thump the pulpit when he got excited; and when he got more excited still he would lean over the pulpit, his face all white, and talk so low and solemn that it would just send the most gorgeous thrills through you.

Dick came to Owlwood – that's our place; I hate these explanations – quite a lot, even before Aunt Tommy came. He and Father were chums; they had been in college together and Father said Dick was the best football player he ever knew. Jill and I soon got acquainted with him and this was another uncanny thing. We had never thought it possible to get acquainted with a minister. Jill said she didn't think it proper for a real live minister to be so chummy. But then Jill was a little jealous because Dick and I, being both men, were better friends than he and she could be. He taught me to skate that winter and fence with canes and do long division. I could never understand long division before Dick came, although I was away on in fractions.

Jill has just been in and says I ought to explain that Dick's name wasn't Dick. I do wish Jill would mind her own business. Of course it wasn't. His real name was the Reverend Stephen Richmond, but Jill and I always called him Dick behind his back; it seemed so jolly and venturesome, somehow, to speak of a minister like that. Only we had to be careful not to let Father and Mother hear us. Mother wouldn't even let Father call Dick "Stephen"; she said it would set a bad example of familiarity to the children. Mother is an old darling. She won't believe we're half as bad as we are.

Well, early in May comes Aunt Tommy. I must explain who Aunt Tommy is or Jill will be at me again. She is Father's youngest sister and her real name is Bertha Gordon, but Father has always called her Tommy and she likes it.

Jill and I had never seen Aunt Tommy before, but we took to her from the start because she was so pretty and because she talked to us just as if we were grown up. She called Jill Elizabeth, and Jill would adore a Hottentot who called her Elizabeth.

Aunt Tommy is the prettiest girl I ever saw. If Jill is half as good-looking when she gets to be twenty – she's only ten now, same age as I am, we're twins – I shall be proud of her for a sister.

Aunt Tommy is all white and dimpled. She has curly red hair and big jolly brown eyes and scrumptious freckles. I do like freckles in a girl, although Jill goes wild if she thinks she has one on her nose. When we talked of writing this story Jill said I wasn't to say that Aunt Tommy had freckles because it wouldn't sound romantic. But I don't care. She has freckles and I think they are all right.

We went to church with Aunt Tommy the first Sunday after she came, one on each side of her. Aunt Tommy is the only girl in the world I'd walk hand in hand with before people. She looked fine that day. She had on a gorgeous dress, all frills and ruffles, and a big white floppy hat. I was proud of her for an aunt, I can tell you, and I was anxious for Dick to see her. When he came up to speak to me and Jill after church came out I said, "Aunt Tommy, this is Mr. Richmond," just like the grown-up people say. Aunt Tommy and Dick shook hands and Dick got as red as anything. It was funny to see him.

The very next evening he came down to Owlwood. We hadn't expected him until Tuesday, for he never came Monday night before. That is Father's night for going to a lodge meeting. Mother was away this time too. I met Dick on the porch and took him into the parlour, thinking what a bully talk we could have all alone together, without Jill bothering around. But in a minute Aunt Tommy came in and she and Dick began to talk, and I just couldn't get a word in edgewise. I got so disgusted I started out, but I don't believe they ever noticed I was gone. I liked Aunt Tommy very well, but I didn't think she had any business to monopolize Dick like that when he and I were such old chums.

Outside I came across Jill. She was sitting all alone in the dark, curled up on the edge of the verandah just where she could see into the parlour through the big glass door. I sat down beside her, for I wanted sympathy.

"Dick's in there talking to Aunt Tommy," I said. "I don't see what makes him want to talk to her."

"What a goose you are!" said Jill in that aggravatingly patronizing way of hers. "Why, Dick has fallen in love with Aunt Tommy!"

Honest, I jumped. I never was so surprised.

"How do you know?" I asked.

"Because I do," said Jill. "I knew it yesterday at church and I think it is so romantic."

"I don't see how you can tell," I said – and I didn't.

"You'll understand better when you get older," said Jill. Sometimes Jill talks as if she were a hundred years older than I am, instead of being a twin. And really, sometimes I think she *is* older.

"I didn't think ministers ever fell in love," I protested.

"Some do," said Jill sagely. "Mr. Grinnell wouldn't ever, I suppose. But Dick is different. I'd like him for a husband myself. But he'd be too old for me by the time I grew up, so I suppose I'll have to let Aunt Tommy have him. It will be all in the family anyhow – that is one comfort. I think Aunt Tommy ought to have me for a flower girl and I'll wear pink silk clouded over with white chiffon and carry a big bouquet of roses."

"Jill, you take my breath away," I said, and she did. My imagination couldn't travel as fast as that. But after I had thought the idea over a bit I liked it. It was a good deal like a book; and, besides, a minister is a respectable thing to have in a family.

"We must help them all we can," said Jill.

"What can we do?" I asked.

"We must praise Dick to Aunt Tommy and Aunt Tommy to Dick and we must keep out of the way – we mustn't ever hang around when they want to be alone," said Jill.

"I don't want to give up being chums with Dick," I grumbled.

"We must be self-sacrificing," said Jill. And that sounded so fine it reconciled me to the attempt.

We sat there and watched Dick and Aunt Tommy for an hour. I thought they were awfully prim and stiff. If I'd been Dick I'd have gone over and hugged her. I said so to Jill and Jill was shocked. She said it wouldn't be proper when they weren't even engaged.

When Dick went away Aunt Tommy came out to the verandah and discovered us. She sat down between us and put her arms about us. Aunt Tommy has such cute ways.

"I like your minister very much," she said.

"He's bully," I said.

"He's as handsome as a prince," Jill said.

"He preaches splendid sermons – he makes people sit up in church, I can tell you," I said.

"He has a heavenly tenor voice," Jill said.

"He's got a magnificent muscle," I said.

"He has the most poetical eyes," Jill said.

"He swims like a duck," I said.

"He looks just like a Greek god," Jill said.

I'm sure Jill couldn't have known what a Greek god looked like, but I suppose she got the comparison out of some novel. Jill is always reading novels. She borrows them from the cook.

Aunt Tommy laughed and said, "You darlings."

For the next three months Jill and I were wild. It was just like reading a serial story to watch Dick and Aunt Tommy. One day when Dick came Aunt Tommy wasn't quite ready to come down, so Jill and I went in to the parlour to help things along. We knew we hadn't much time, so we began right off.

"Aunt Tommy is the jolliest girl I know," I said.

"She is as beautiful as a dream," Jill said.

"She can play games as good as a boy," I said.

"She does the most elegant fancy work," Jill said.

"She never gets mad," I said.

"She plays and sings divinely," Jill said.

"She can cook awfully good things," I said, for I was beginning to run short of compliments. Jill was horrified; she said afterwards that it wasn't a bit romantic. But I don't care – I believe Dick liked it, for he smiled with his eyes just as he always does when he's pleased. Girls don't understand everything.

BUT AT THE END OF THREE MONTHS we began to get anxious. Things were going so slow. Dick and Aunt Tommy didn't seem a bit further ahead than at first. Jill said it was because Aunt Tommy didn't encourage Dick enough.

"I do wish we could hurry them up a little," she said. "At this rate they will never be married this year and by next I'll be too big to be a flower girl. I'm stretching out horribly as it is. Mother has had to let down my frocks again."

"I wish they would get engaged and have done with it," I said. "My mind would be at rest then. It's all Dick's fault. Why doesn't he ask Aunt Tommy to marry him? What's making him so slow about it? If I wanted a girl to marry me – but I wouldn't ever – I'd tell her so right spang off."

"I suppose ministers have to be more dignified," said Jill, "but three months ought to be enough time for anyone. And Aunt Tommy is only going to be here another month. If Dick could be made a little jealous it would hurry him up. And he could be made jealous if you had any spunk about you."

"I guess I've got more spunk than you have," I said.

"The trouble with Dick is this," said Jill. "There is nobody else coming to see Aunt Tommy and he thinks he is sure of her. If you could tell him something different it would stir him up."

"Are you sure it would?" I asked.

"It always does in novels," said Jill. And that settled it, of course.

Jill and I fixed up what I was to say and Jill made me say it over and over again to be sure I had it right. I told her – sarcastically – that she'd better say it herself and then it would be done properly. Jill said she would if it were Aunt Tommy, but when it was Dick it was better for a man to do it. So of course I agreed.

I didn't know when I would have a chance to stir Dick up, but Providence – so Jill said – favoured us. Aunt Tommy didn't expect Dick down the next night, so she and Father and Mother all went away somewhere. Dick came after all, and Jill sent me into the parlour to tell him. He was standing before the mantel looking at Aunt Tommy's picture. There was such an adoring look in his eyes. I could see it quite plain in the mirror before him. I practised that look a lot before my own glass after that – because I thought it might come in handy some time, you know – but I guess I couldn't have got it just right because when I tried it on Jill she asked me if I had a pain.

"Well, Jack, old man," said Dick, sitting down on the sofa. I sat down before him.

"Aunt Tommy is out," I said, to get the worst over. "I guess you like Aunt Tommy pretty well, don't you, Mr. Richmond?"

"Yes," said Dick softly.

"So do other men," I said – mysterious, as Jill had ordered me.

Dick thumped one of the sofa pillows.

"Yes, I suppose so," he said.

"There's a man in New York who just worships Aunt Tommy," I said. "He writes her most every day and sends her books and music and elegant presents. I guess she's pretty fond of him too. She keeps his photograph on her bedroom table and I've seen her kissing it."

I stopped there, not because I had said all I had to say, but because Dick's face scared me – honest, it did. It had all gone white, like it does in the pulpit sometimes when he is tremendously in earnest, only ten times worse. But all he said was,

"Is your Aunt Bertha engaged to this – this man?"

"Not exactly engaged," I said, "but I guess anybody else who wants to marry her will have to reckon with him."

Dick got up.

"I think I won't wait this evening," he said.

"I wish you'd stay and have a talk with me," I said. "I haven't had a talk with you for ages and I have a million things to tell you."

Dick smiled as if it hurt him to smile.

"I can't tonight, Jacky. Some other time we'll have a good powwow, old chap."

He took his hat and went out. Then Jill came flying in to hear all about it. I told her as well as I could, but she wasn't satisfied. If Dick took it so quietly, she declared, I couldn't have made it strong enough.

"If you had seen Dick's face," I said, "you would have thought I made it plenty strong. And I'd like to know what Aunt Tommy will say to all this when she finds out."

"Well, you didn't tell a thing but what was true," said Jill.

The next evening was Dick's regular night for coming, but he didn't come, although Jill and I went down the lane a dozen times to watch for him. The night after that was prayer-meeting night. Dick had always walked home with Aunt Tommy and us, but that night he didn't. He only just bowed and smiled as he passed us in the porch. Aunt Tommy hardly spoke all the way home, only just held tight to Jill's and my hands. But after we got home she seemed in great spirits and laughed and chatted with Father and Mother.

"What does this mean?" asked Jill, grabbing me in the hall on our way to bed.

"You'd better get another novel from the cook and find out," I said grouchily. I was disgusted with things in general and Dick in particular.

The three weeks that followed were awful. Dick never came near Owlwood. Jill and I fought every day, we were so cross and disappointed. Nothing had come out right, and Jill blamed it all on me. She said I must have made it too strong. There was no fun in anything, not even in going to church. Dick hardly thumped the pulpit at all and when he did it was only a measly little thump. But Aunt Tommy didn't seem to worry any. She sang and laughed and joked from morning to night.

"She doesn't mind Dick's making an ass of himself, anyway, that's one consolation," I said to Jill.

"She is breaking her heart about it," said Jill, "and that's your consolation!"

"I don't believe it," I said. "What makes you think so?"

"She cries every night," said Jill. "I can tell by the look of her eyes in the morning."

"She doesn't look half as woebegone over it as you do," I said.

"If I had her reason for looking woebegone I wouldn't look it either," said Jill.

I asked her to explain her meaning, but she only said that little boys couldn't understand those things.

Things went on like this for another week. Then they

reached – so Jill says – a climax. If Jill knows what that means I don't. But Pinky Carewe was the climax. Pinky's name is James, but Jill and I always called him Pinky because we couldn't bear him. He took to calling at Owlwood and one evening he took Aunt Tommy out driving. Then Jill came to me.

"Something has got to be done," she said resolutely. "I am not going to have Pinky Carewe for an Uncle Tommy and that is all there is about it. You must go straight to Dick and tell him the truth about the New York man."

I looked at Jill to see if she were in earnest. When I saw that she was I said, "I wouldn't take all the gems of Golconda and go and tell Dick that I'd been hoaxing him. You can do it yourself, Jill Gordon."

"You didn't tell him anything that wasn't true," said Jill.

"I don't know how a minister might look upon it," I said. "Anyway, I won't go."

"Then I suppose I've got to," said Jill very dolefully.

"Yes, you'll have to," I said.

And this finishes my part of the story, and Jill is going to tell the rest. But you needn't believe everything she says about me in it.

Jill's Side of It

Jacky has made a fearful muddle of his part, but I suppose I shall just have to let it go. You couldn't expect much better of a boy. But I am determined to re-describe Aunt Tommy, for the way Jacky has done it is just disgraceful. I know exactly how to do it, the way it is always done in stories.

Aunt Tommy is divinely beautiful. Her magnificent wealth of burnished auburn hair flows back in amethystine waves from her sun-kissed brow. Her eyes are gloriously dark and deep, like midnight lakes mirroring the stars of heaven;

her features are like sculptured marble and her mouth is like a trembling, curving Cupid's bow (this is a classical allusion) luscious and glowing as a dewy rose. Her creamy skin is as fair and flawless as the inner petals of a white lily. (She may have a weeny teeny freckle or two in summer, but you'd never notice.) Her slender form is matchless in its symmetry and her voice is like the ripple of a woodland brook.

There, I'm sure that's ever so much better than Jacky's description, and now I can proceed with a clear conscience.

Well, I didn't like the idea of going and explaining to Dick very much, but it had to be done unless I wanted to run the risk of having Pinky Carewe in the family. So I went the next morning.

I put on my very prettiest pink organdie dress and did my hair the new way, which is very becoming to me. When you are going to have an important interview with a man it is always well to look your very best. I put on my big hat with the wreath of pink roses that Aunt Tommy had brought me from New York and took my spandy ruffled parasol.

"With your shield or upon it, Jill," said Jacky when I started. (This is another classical allusion.)

I went straight up the hill and down the road to the manse where Dick lived with his old housekeeper, Mrs. Dodge. She came to the door when I knocked and I said, very politely, "Can I see the Reverend Stephen Richmond, if you please?"

Mrs. Dodge went upstairs and came right back saying would I please go up to the study. Up I went, my heart in my mouth, I can tell you, and there was Dick among his books, looking so pale and sorrowful and interesting, for all the world like Lord Algernon Francis in the splendid serial in the paper cook took. There was a Madonna on his desk that looked just like Aunt Tommy.

"Good evening, Miss Elizabeth," said Dick, just as if I were grown up, you know. "Won't you sit down? Try that green velvet chair. I am sure it was created for a pink dress and unfortunately neither Mrs. Dodge nor I possess one. How are all your people?"

"We are all pretty well, thank you," I said, "except Aunt Tommy. She –" I was going to say, "She cries every night after she goes to bed," but I remembered just in time that if I were in Aunt Tommy's place I wouldn't want a man to know I cried about him even if I did. So I said instead "– she has got a cold."

"Ah, indeed, I am sorry to hear it," said Dick, politely but coldly, as if it were part of his duty as a minister to be sorry for anybody who had a cold, but as if, apart from that, it was no concern of his if Aunt Tommy had galloping consumption.

"And Jack and I are terribly harrowed up in our minds," I went on. "That is what I've come up to see you about."

"Well, tell me all about it," said Dick.

"I'm afraid to," I said. "I know you'll be cross even if you are a minister. It's about what Jack told you about that man in New York and Aunt Tommy."

Dick turned as red as fire.

"I'd rather not discuss your Aunt Bertha's affairs," he said stiffly.

"You *must* hear this," I cried, feeling thankful that Jacky hadn't come after all, for he'd never have got any further ahead after that snub. "It's all a mistake. There is a man in New York and he just worships Aunt Tommy and she just adores him. But he's seventy years old and he's her Uncle Matthew who brought her up ever since her father died and you've heard her talking about him a hundred times. That's all, cross my heart solemn and true."

You never saw anything like Dick's face when I stopped. It looked just like a sunrise. But he said slowly, "Why did Jacky tell me such a – tell me it in such a way?"

"We wanted to make you jealous," I said. "I put Jacky up to it."

"I didn't think it was in either of you to do such a thing," said Dick reproachfully.

"Oh, Dick," I cried – fancy my calling him Dick right to his face! Jacky will never believe I really did it. He says I would never have dared. But it wasn't daring at all, it was just forgetting. "Oh, Dick, we didn't mean any harm. We thought you weren't getting on fast enough and we wanted to stir you up like they do in books. We thought if we made you jealous it would work all right. We didn't mean any harm. Oh, please forgive us!"

I was just ready to cry. But that dear Dick leaned over the table and patted my hand.

"There, there, it's all right. I understand and of course I forgive you. Don't cry, sweetheart."

The way Dick said "sweetheart" was perfectly lovely. I envied Aunt Tommy, and I wanted to keep on crying so that he would go on comforting me.

"And you'll come back to see Aunt Tommy again?" I said.

Dick's face clouded over; he got up and walked around the room several times before he said a word. Then he came and sat down beside me and explained it all to me, just as if I were grown up.

"Sweetheart, we'll talk this all out. You see, it is this way. Your Aunt Bertha is the sweetest woman in the world. But I'm only a poor minister and I have no right to ask her to share my life of hard work and self-denial. And even if I dared I know she wouldn't do it. She doesn't care anything for me except as a friend. I never meant to tell her I cared for her but I couldn't help going to Owlwood, even though I knew it was a weakness on my part. So now that I'm out of the habit of going I think it would be wisest to stay out. It hurts dreadfully, but it would hurt worse after a while. Don't you agree with me, Miss Elizabeth?"

I thought hard and fast. If I were in Aunt Tommy's place I mightn't want a man to know I cried about him, but I was quite sure I'd rather have him know than have him stay away because he didn't know. So I spoke right up.

"No, I don't, Mr. Richmond. Aunt Tommy does care – you just ask her. She cries every blessed night because you never come to Owlwood."

"Oh, Elizabeth!" said Dick.

He got up and stalked about the room again.

"You'll come back?" I said.

"Yes," he answered.

I drew a long breath. It was such a responsibility off my mind.

"Then you'd better come down with me right off," I said, "for Pinky Carewe had her out driving last night and I want a stop put to that as soon as possible. Even if he is rich he's a perfect pig."

Dick got his hat and came. We walked up the road in a lovely creamy yellow twilight and I was, oh, so happy.

"Isn't it just like a novel?" I said.

"I am afraid, Elizabeth," said Dick preachily, "that you read too many novels, and not the right kind, either. Some of these days I am going to ask you to promise me that you will read no more books except those your mother and I pick out for you."

You don't know how squelched I felt. And I knew I would have to promise, too, for Dick can make me do anything he likes.

When we got to Owlwood I left Dick in the parlour and flew up to Aunt Tommy's room. I found her all scrunched up on her bed in the dark with her face in the pillows.

"Aunt Tommy, Dick is down in the parlour and he wants to see you," I said.

Didn't Aunt Tommy fly up, though!

"Oh, Jill – but I'm not fit to be seen – tell him I'll be down in a few minutes."

I knew Aunt Tommy wanted to fix her hair and dab rose-water on her eyes, so I trotted meekly down and told Dick. Then I flew out to Jacky and dragged him around to the glass door. It was all hung over with vines and a wee bit ajar so that we could see and hear everything that went on.

Jacky said it was only sneaks that listened – but he didn't say it until next day. At the time he listened just as hard as I did. I didn't care if it was mean. I just had to listen. I was perfectly wild to hear how a man would propose and how a girl would accept and it was too good a chance to lose.

Presently in sweeps Aunt Tommy, in an elegant dress, not a hair out of place. She looked perfectly sweet, only her nose was a little red. Dick looked at her for just a moment, then he stepped forward and took her right into his arms.

Aunt Tommy drew back her head for just a second as if she were going to crush him in the dust, and then she just all kind of crumpled up and her face went down on his shoulder.

"Oh – Bertha – I – love – you – I – love you," he said, just like that, all quick and jerky.

"You – you have taken a queer way of showing it," said Aunt Tommy, all muffled.

"I – I – was led to believe that there was another man – whom you cared for – and I thought you were only trifling with me. So I sulked like a jealous fool. Bertha, darling, you do love me a little, don't you?"

Aunt Tommy lifted her head and stuck up her mouth and he kissed her. And there it was, all over, and they were engaged as quick as that, mind you. He didn't even go down on his knees. There was nothing romantic about it and I was never so disgusted in my life. When I grow up and anybody proposes to me he will have to be a good deal more flowery and eloquent than that, I can tell you, if he wants me to listen to him.

I left Jacky peeking still and I went to bed. After a long time Aunt Tommy came up to my room and sat down on my bed in the moonlight.

"You dear blessed Elizabeth!" she said.

"It's all right then, is it?" I asked.

"Yes, it is all right, thanks to you, dearie. We are to be married in October and somebody must be my little flower girl."

"I think Dick will make a splendid husband," I said. "But, Aunt Tommy, you mustn't be too hard on Jacky. He only wanted to help things along, and it was I who put him up to it in the first place."

"You have atoned by going and confessing," said Aunt Tommy with a hug. "Jacky had no business to put that off on you. I'll forgive him, of course, but I'll punish him by not letting him know that I will for a little while. Then I'll ask him to be a page at my wedding."

Well, the wedding came off last week. It was a perfectly gorgeous affair. Aunt Tommy's dress was a dream – and so was mine, all pink silk and chiffon and carnations. Jacky made a magnificent page too, in a suit of white velvet. The wedding cake was four stories high, and Dick looked perfectly handsome. He kissed me too, right after he kissed Aunt Tommy.

So everything turned out all right, and I believe Dick would never have dared to speak up if we hadn't helped things along. But Jacky and I have decided that we will never meddle in an affair of the kind again. It is too hard on the nerves.

Afterword: Finding L. M. Montgomery's Short Stories

GREAT LITERARY FINDS are not exactly a dime-a-dozen. But even if they were, for the finder they would always be exciting. I had no notion of ever being one of those people who find something interesting in their own or someone else's attic. In fact, I never thought of looking. When a friend and I visited L. M. Montgomery's birthplace in New London, P.E.I., in 1977, we were going simply as interested tourists, tourists interested in the author of the twenty books that began with *Anne of Green Gables.* It was my friend who called me over to a glass-fronted display cabinet to look at a short story pasted in a scrapbook. Did I know it? Silly question. Didn't I know all her twenty novels and four short story collections almost off by heart by virtue of constant re-reading since the age of eleven? Of course I would know this story. But I didn't.

Luckily, the ladies in charge weren't particularly busy and were pleased to get the scrapbook out of the case for me. It was full of short stories by Montgomery, none of which I had ever seen before. "Well, if you're really interested, there are more upstairs," they told me. Up the stairs, in one of the tiny bedrooms, was a cardboard box, the floor around it sprinkled with Mouse Feast. There were eleven other scrapbooks in the box; all contained clippings of published stories and poems by L. M. Montgomery. A feast indeed, but for mice? Were these collections safe, kept in a cardboard box, in a frame house, surrounded by Mouse Feast? I found out much later that the stories only visited the birthplace in the summer and were carried off to the Confederation Centre archives in Charlottetown at the end of the season. But at the time my concern was that they survive until I could come back with more time and read them all.

That was my original focus. I wanted to read them. Unlike most young women who had read *Anne* and the other novels in their teens and then put them aside as childish things, I never stopped reading them. I read them year in and year out, again and again. I never tired of their apparent simplicity, finding them more complex than they seemed, their emotions true and believable. They were part of my innermost being. But there weren't enough of them. Only twenty novels and forty-eight short stories.

Now here was a collection of hundreds. How many, I had not time on that visit to discover. But I knew that I must make sure they were safe, and that I must get permission from someone to look through and read them all and, if possible, copy them so I could go on re-reading them too. Still, it took me a while to get up my courage to do anything about it. Surely, I thought, it must be just my ignorance that I didn't know about these collections; probably everyone in the field (was there a Montgomery field in 1977?) knew about them. And might I tread on academic toes?

One thing I did know was that Montgomery's younger son, Dr. Stuart Macdonald, lived in Toronto, but I thought that he was probably constantly pestered by Montgomery fans and that I should not intrude on him. Without contacting him, I did go back to P.E.I. the next summer and spent a happy couple of days making a list of every story and poem in all twelve collections. Only about half of the collections, by the way, were bound scrapbooks, into which were pasted the pieces Montgomery had clipped. The other half were sewn gatherings of full pages from magazines. I even read a few of the stories, but again, time was short.

Back home in Toronto I put together a typed pamphlet called "A Listing of Scrapbooks and Gatherings in Montgomery's Birthplace," put a spiral binding on it, and called it a private publication (1978). This seemed rather respectable (it was 27 pages long and contained over 700 entries, half of them poems, the other half stories), so I summoned up the courage to write to Dr. Macdonald. He answered most kindly. He had been unaware of the existence of the stories and, once I had proved my sincere intentions, was willing that I should have access to them. He arranged that his friend Father Francis Bolger, a professor at the University of Prince Edward Island and a trustee of the birthplace, have them photocopied. (Father Bolger was familiar with the collection of scrapbooks because he had used their contents for his book about Montgomery's early publications, *The Years before "Anne"*.) The process of copying took about a year, because only one scrapbook at a time could be removed from the collection. Father Bolger made two copies of the scrapbooks, keeping one for the University of Prince Edward Island archives and sending one to me; on receipt of the second copy I made a set for Dr. Macdonald, which went to the University of Guelph archives on his death.

What an orgy of reading I had that year! I revelled in every new story, whether it was good or not so good. Some stories were exceptional; some had obviously been churned out at top speed. Several seemed familiar; they were the originals of vignettes in some of the novels. ("Mrs. Skinner's Story," published in *Westminster Magazine* in 1907, was adapted for Chapter 30 of *Anne of the Island* in 1915; "A House Divided against Itself," published in *Canadian Home Journal* in 1930, became one of the strands in *A Tangled Web* the very next year; *Anne of Windy Poplars* and *Anne of Ingleside* are made up almost wholly of stories that had first seen the light of day previously.) Some stories appeared more than once, having been sold, with few or no alterations, to different magazines. Some had Montgomery's own handwritten corrections of typographical errors and stylistic adjustments. All were interesting to me as showing the range of her talent and her ability to keep at it. Does one today assume that every newspaper writer will produce gems of stylistic brilliance in every column, every day? Of course not. And that is almost the way Montgomery was writing: at that speed and at that volume. But more of the volume later.

There was just enough publication information (magazine names and dates) attached to the stories in the sewn gatherings to make me want to produce a bibliography. The 360 stories of which I now had copies had been published in 134 different magazines and newspapers, running from the *Advocate and Guardian* to *Zion's Herald,* and covering most of the rest of the alphabet in between. Of course I couldn't find all these magazines. Some were tiny affairs, long since deceased. Some were ephemeral Sunday School publications. But in the Library of Congress in Washington, D.C., in the New York Public Library, the Toronto Public Library, and a few other regional libraries, I tracked down many of them. They had no indexes, of course. No tables of contents. I spent many hours in the stacks of the Library of Congress leafing through enormous bound volumes of *Boys' World* and *Girls' Companion,* freezing my bottom on cold marble floors and covering my top with decaying leather. And every so often, in the midst of keeping track of dates and page numbers, I would find a story not in the scrapbook collections. Eventually my filing cabinet contained over 400 items.

You might think that, with 400 items, I must surely have a complete collection. Not so. Dr. Macdonald let me borrow and copy a ledger Montgomery had kept, in which she listed every dollar she had earned from her publications: stories, poems, and novels. Her list of stories reached No. 517. Reading the list carefully, I discovered that some of those 517 were chapters of books: *Magic for Marigold* and *Emily of New Moon*, for instance, came out serially (the former before, the latter after, publication as a novel), and Montgomery listed those chapters as short stories in her list. To add a little confusion, sometimes Montgomery's numbers got out of order: she would misread a seven as a one and continue with two rather than with eight, thereby repeating numbers already used, or she would do the opposite, jumping from one to eight, having misread the one as a seven. Some of the stories I had were not on her list; others she did list were not in the scrapbooks and I had not found them. Still, when I completed the bibliography in 1985, listing the found and unfound stories, there were 506 titles, and copies of 400 of them were in my collection. I will probably never find the other 106 stories.

All this time, Mary Rubio and Elizabeth Waterston of the University of Guelph had been comforters and sustainers. They had published my first article, a preliminary bibliography of the stories, in *Canadian Children's Literature* in 1983. They had encouraged me, nay, ordered me, to apply for a Canada Council grant to complete the bibliography. Now they leaned on me again: "Get the stories out to the public." Dr. Macdonald had died since my work began, but he had often expressed his hope that I could get some of the stories published. And so I approached McClelland and Stewart in 1985. They accepted my proposal for the first collection of stories, and *Akin to Anne: Tales of Other Orphans* came out three years later. The next three followed year by year: *Along the Shore: Tales by the Sea*, *Among the Shadows: Tales from the Darker Side*, and *After Many Days: Tales of Time Passed.* A fifth, *Against the Odds: Tales of Achievement*, appeared in the spring of 1993; this collection, *At the Altar: Matrimonial*

Tales, the sixth, in 1994. I hope there will be at least two or three more collections.

I have often been asked why the collections have been grouped thematically. As I was reading over the stories to choose those worth publishing they seemed to fall naturally into certain categories, and although it makes for some sameness to have nineteen stories all about orphans, it is also interesting to note the changes Montgomery is able to ring on such a theme. A chronological presentation or a "best of" collection would pose other problems, so the theme decision was adhered to.

I mentioned before that I had been struck, on first reading the photocopies of the scrapbooks through, at finding stories that I recognized from the novels. But even when Montgomery repeats a story or recycles a plot from one story to another, she finds ways in her use of character and setting and point of view to vary it. She was, after all, a professional writer; she wrote in order to earn money; and she produced stories in a quantity that is somewhat staggering. Her output of novels is just as amazing, considering that, as she was producing them, she was a minister's wife in a small Ontario community, with all the duties that position used to entail. And if there is a distinct falling off in the last two *Anne* books, written at her publisher's insistence, when she was sick of Anne, *Jane of Lantern Hill*, her last book, is one of her best.

Montgomery's first poem was published in 1890; her first story in 1895. In 1901, 13 stories and 28 poems appeared; in 1903, the high point for poems, 32; in 1905, the high point for stories, 44. By 1910, when her novel-writing began to take precedence, her output of stories was down to nine (but another 22, previously published, were re-published); 12 new poems and five re-publications of poems came out that year. An amazing record, and an amazing woman.

Since the publication of her journals, for which we are all

eternally grateful to Mary Rubio and Elizabeth Waterston, Montgomery seems much more interesting as a person and worthy of attention as a writer. Is it because we now know of the occasional despair that lay behind the sweetness and light of most of her writing? There are depths to Montgomery, as scholars, critics, and readers are increasingly coming to discover.

REA WILMSHURST

Editorial Note

The stories in this collection were originally published in the following magazines and newspapers, and are listed here in alphabetical order. Dates in square brackets are conjectural. Where the original illustrations accompanying the stories are available, they have been included. Obvious typographical errors have been corrected, spelling and punctuation normalized.

Aunt Philippa and the Men, *Red Book Magazine*, January 1915, 518–24.

By the Rule of Contrary, *Farm and Fireside*, 10 July 1908, 15.

A Dinner of Herbs, *Chatelaine*, October 1928, 10–11, 40.

The Dissipation of Miss Ponsonby, *Housewife*, February 1906, 1–2.

The Gossip of Valley View, *National Magazine*, February 1910, 534–38.

Jessamine, *Household Dealer* [1900]; also in *Farm and Fireside*, June 1909, 14–15.

Miss Cordelia's Accommodation, *American Young People* [1903].

Nan [1904]. Text from a Montgomery scrapbook; no other details available.

Them Notorious Pigs, in *American Agriculturist* and *New England Homestead*, both October 1904, 335–36, 339, as "The Nuisance of Women."

The Penningtons' Girl, *Ladies' Journal* [1900].
The Pursuit of the Ideal, *What To Eat*, May 1904, 145–47.
The Touch of Fate, *Unique Monthly* [1899].
The Twins and a Wedding, *Holland's Magazine*, May 1908, 12–13; also in *MacLean's*, September 1915, 22–24, 84; and as "The Twins and a Pretty Wedding," *Springfield Republican*, May 1910, 26.
An Unconventional Confidence, *Designer*, n.d.; also in *New Idea Woman's Magazine*, April 1903, 20–22; and in *Canadian Courier*, April 1912, 32–33.
The Way of the Winning of Anne, *Springfield Republican*, December 1899, 18; also (anon.) as "The Winning of Anne," *Family Herald*, May 1900, 22.
What Aunt Marcella Would Have Called It, *Family Herald*, June 1935, 19.
When Jack and Jill Took a Hand, *Gunter's Magazine*, October 1905, 370–78; also in *MacLean's*, March 1915, 20–22, 91–94.
The Wooing of Bessy, *Trotwood's Monthly*, April 1906, 367–71.

Acknowledgements

The late Dr. Stuart Macdonald gave me permission to begin the research that culminated in my collection of Montgomery's stories; Professors Mary Rubio and Elizabeth Waterston encouraged and advised me; C. Anderson Silber gave his constant support. Librarians were unfailingly helpful.

OTHER BOOKS BY

L. M. Montgomery

For the most complete listing, see Russell, Russell, and Wilmshurst, *Lucy Maud Montgomery: A Preliminary Bibliography*, University of Waterloo Library Bibliography Series, No. 13 (Waterloo: University of Waterloo Library, 1986).

The "Anne" Books (in order of Anne's life)

Anne of Green Gables, 1908
Anne of Avonlea, 1909
Anne of the Island, 1915
Anne of Windy Poplars, 1936
Anne's House of Dreams, 1917
Anne of Ingleside, 1939
Rainbow Valley, 1919
Rilla of Ingleside, 1920

The "Emily" Books

Emily of New Moon, 1923
Emily Climbs, 1925
Emily's Quest, 1927

Other Novels (in chronological order)

Kilmeny of the Orchard, 1910
The Story Girl, 1911
The Golden Road, 1913
The Blue Castle, 1926
Magic for Marigold, 1929
A Tangled Web, 1931
Pat of Silver Bush, 1933
Mistress Pat, 1935
Jane of Lantern Hill, 1937

Collections of Short Stories

Chronicles of Avonlea, 1912
Further Chronicles of Avonlea, 1920
The Road to Yesterday, 1974
The Doctor's Sweetheart, and Other Stories, 1979
Akin to Anne: Tales of Other Orphans, 1988
Along the Shore: Tales by the Sea, 1989
Among the Shadows: Tales from the Darker Side, 1990
After Many Days: Tales of Time Passed, 1991
Against the Odds: Tales of Achievement, 1993

Poetry

The Watchman, and Other Poems, 1916
Poetry of Lucy Maud Montgomery, 1987